KEEPING

LONG ISLAND

Courtney Peppernell

Acknowledgements

This novel would not have been possible without the support, guidance and encouragement of the following people and institutions:

James De'Bono
Emma Batting
Alexandria M. Warneke
Polgarus Studio
Jelzoo Digital Publishing
Sea Life Aquarium
Long Island Aquarium and Exhibition Center
My friends and family

And to my partner Rhian – thank you for always being an honest critic and for believing in me.

Dear You,
Your softness will always be needed in this world.
Love,
The Author

fall

semester one

August 30, 2012

Dear Keeper,

My name is Kayden, and if my heart holds any more secrets, it might collapse. At least this is what my therapist says. Today she told me to buy a notebook. She didn't specify what kind of notebook, so I bought one with lots of pages because I liked the pattern on the front. She told me that it's good to share and that the notebook will hold all my thoughts. I asked her if she meant like a secret keeper and she said yes. I like the idea of a secret keeper, someone who keeps secrets safe when you're too tired to carry the weight on your own. Maybe one day I can show all of this to somebody. So I guess if you are reading this, I hope you don't mind me sharing. I'm just trying to do what my therapist thinks will help, so I don't become stuck again. I do want to be able to share again or least *start* sharing – I've never been very good at it. I just lock all my thoughts away, and they build up over time until they are so loud it feels like I might explode. It doesn't matter how many times I try to talk about things, I just can't seem to figure out how to say them. I know this is because things take time and big things take even more time, but I am afraid because things used to be very bad. And I feel strange because I have plenty of friends to talk to, and my dad always tries to talk to me, but I don't *feel* like I can talk to any of them. Do you feel like that sometimes? Like you're surrounded by people but you feel alone? It's very confusing. I just want to know that there is someone out there who will listen to my secrets and not think I'm weird.

I will be graduating college soon. I think that means I should have some idea of how my life should go, but if I'm honest, I don't. My mom and I barely talk, and lately my dad has been extra worried about me. It's been years but they still can't have a conversation that doesn't involve arguing over me. I wish they were a normal divorced couple almost as much as I wish I didn't have so many freckles and my hands didn't shake when I'm nervous. I went on a date a few weeks ago, but I was told I was too soft. I didn't even want to go on the date in the first place but my dad said maybe someone new would be good for me. He was wrong.

I know that it's my fault because I've built too many walls around my heart. But sometimes I like to imagine someone breaking down these walls, slowly chipping away until they find me on the other side. I wonder what kind of person that would be or if they even exist.

When I was in high school I lost someone, and I wish she were still alive but she's not, and maybe that's the reason why the world has become such a hard place to live in. I try not to feel sad, but the sadness keeps coming back like an old friend and we've never said goodbye to each other. My anxiety isn't as bad these days, but in high school it was so bad that sometimes the only thing that could calm me down was a small portable radio I own. My pop gave it to me when I was little and it makes me feel safe. I never leave the house without it, even if there is only one frequency that works. It's an old radio station that not many people listen to these days. I like to think I am their lone listener. Just me and every song. I wish my friends understood me the way music does. I don't want people to give up on me, but I barely say anything these days, and that's enough reason to give up on someone, I think. I hope you don't give up on me. I know we've just met, but I really need someone to believe in me.

It's 3am. I finished reading an online article about natural selection earlier and then I called my best friend. There was lots of silence and he kept asking me if I was okay. I don't know why I said I was fine when I know that I'm not. I also don't know why I stayed up to write you all this. I guess I just felt like it. I start my final year of college next week. I am not sure how I am going to do that with all these loud thoughts in my head, but if I have you to share them with, maybe everything will be fine again.

Thanks for listening,
Kayden

September 3, 2012

Dear Keeper,

My truck broke down on the way to class and I cried about it. I don't know why I cried about it, I just did. I always cry over everything lately, maybe that's how my dad can tell it's getting bad again. It's always been bad, it's just that I got good at pretending. Lately I'm too tired to pretend, and I think people are noticing. It was the first day back after all. It was just bad luck. I called Nate and he picked me up and then he laughed because my truck always breaks down. I suppose it was a little funny. Nate's my best friend. He's the only person I would cry in front of other than my therapist. I met Nate during my first year of college. He told me he thought I was cool because I was weird. I think he misunderstood weird for sad but I've never told him that. My last year of high school was such a bad time. I hate talking about it. I hate even thinking about it. But I guess that this is the point of you, so that I can start sharing. After finishing high school and my parents splitting up, I moved from Colorado to East Point, Long Island to live with my dad and go to college. Back then, I had asked him if he thought I was running away from everything, and he said he thought I was just starting again. Everyone deserves to start again, right?

I tried really hard in the first year of college not to be sad. I made friends because my dad said it would help distract me. I spent hours in the library reading books because it was something to fill the time. I asked my professors for extra work, and I even wrote my mom emails. But sometimes there are things you can never forget, no matter how hard you try. I got through freshman year of college by staying busy, and then in my sophomore year, I lost control. My therapist says this is because some people take a while to recognize something traumatic and even longer to heal. I remember one night I was lying on my bedroom floor and my dad walked in. His eyes were puffy and I think he had been crying. He sat on my bed and he told me that he didn't want to lose his daughter. I'll never forget that conversation, it's just something you don't ever forget.

He said, "I can't lose you, too, Kayden. I lost your mother, but I can't lose you."

And I said, "I'm right here, Dad," because I thought I could handle all my thoughts on my own.

"No, you are not," he said back. "Your shell is here, and there is nothing inside anymore."

My dad owns an auto shop. He fixes cars every day. Sometimes there are cars that come in that look immaculate. There are no scratches, no dents, no chips of paint missing. They look brand new. My dad says some people are like those cars. They look well and happy on the outside, but on the inside, they look quite different. All it takes is for someone to crack open the hood and realize that most of the parts are missing. I think I needed someone to open the hood and help me fix the parts that weren't working anymore. My therapist doesn't wear jeans and a t-shirt or have grease smeared on her face and oil under her fingernails, but she is trying to give me the tools to fix what is damaged. I have never told her this, but I will tell you – I'm not sure why I take the tools but never use them.

Maybe today was just chaotic because it was the first day back and it's my final year. I am afraid. I don't know what's going to happen after college. I have been used to getting through day by day, one year after another. It's easier to stay alive when you are just going through the motions: I know what comes next, I know what to say if people ask how I am. But after this year it's all going to change. What if I make a mess of things again? I guess I've been thinking about all this lately because graduation is in 259 days and I *should* start thinking about these things, even if sometimes it might be nicer to lie on my bedroom floor for a hundred years and not think about a single thing other than the changing colors of the sky.

Thanks for listening,
Kayden

September 6, 2012

Dear Keeper,

When I first started therapy three years ago, we used to talk about my parents' divorce. We also talked about my happiest memories. It's hard to think about happy memories when you are trying to shut the bad ones out. Often, they go hand in hand, although I'm not sure why. My happiest memories are probably the ones I have from my early childhood. This was when my parents were happier at least. After that, the memories happen in short bursts and I have to stop thinking because otherwise I start remembering the bad ones, which I don't like to do. My therapist tries to get me to talk about my bad memories all the time. Sometimes I do, sometimes I don't. Before my parents divorced, I thought that love was something that should last forever, but maybe this isn't always true. Sometimes people are not happy with themselves, which means they can't always make each other happy. I used to tell myself that my parents valued each other's happiness and that's why they left each other. It took them nearly my entire childhood to do it, but maybe they thought staying together was the best thing to do for me. It wasn't.

It was bad towards the end, so bad that I thought even I was losing a part of myself. Maybe I was. I realized then that people just fall out of love and there's nothing anyone can do about it, it just happens. Even if my parents fell out of love, I still know what love is like. It makes you feel dizzy and it also makes you feel light and it hurts. It hurts you so much, but you still want it. My parents made each other all these promises and they couldn't keep them. Maybe that's why it's so hard for me to make promises to people. I just don't want to let people down. I hope I don't end up letting you down. I really don't want to do that.

I almost didn't go to my first therapy session. I wasn't sure if it would work, but Nate said that it might, so I went. I caught the train from school to the city where her office is. It's an hour train ride from Long Island but that's okay because I listen to my radio a lot. Her office is tucked away in the inner parts of Lincoln Square. It feels like a castle. Just an endless castle of skyscrapers made of glass, busy people who never slow down, and traffic that builds up in all its pockets. I was trying to get to the heart of the city to figure out where my own heart had gone. The receptionist was very nice and she made me feel like I wasn't a freak. She doesn't work there anymore though. When I walked into the office, I felt uncomfortable. The first thing my therapist said was that she was glad I had come to see her. I told her my friend thought it was a good idea, and the doctors at the hospital couldn't do anything else to help me.

Then she said, "Kayden, this isn't a place to be afraid of."

I said I was afraid, because I was.

And she told me I was in a safe place and she was happy to share the safe place with me.

I will never forget that, especially that word *share.* It's been burned into my brain since that day.

She also made a promise to me in that first session.

"I'm here to listen, Kayden. You just take your time, and I'll listen. That I can promise you." That was the first promise in a really long time that someone actually kept. The only problem now is that it's getting bad again and I am closing up, and the words I want to say to her are not coming out. This might be why she wants me to talk to you. So that I don't have to say the words out loud anymore. I can write them to you instead. I'm trying very hard to let you inside the walls. I just wanted you to know that.

Today's session was okay but it wasn't the best. I feel tired, but she says to keep writing to you and it will help. I am sure it will.

Thanks for listening,
Kayden

September 11, 2012

Dear Keeper,

It takes more than a pulse, a steady heartbeat, and a breath to live. Lately I have been living, but not really. Last week when I wrote to you, I forgot to tell you something that my therapist had asked in our session. She asked me if I was surviving or if I was living. I didn't know there was a difference.

It's my second week of the semester. Today is also the eleventh anniversary of the collapse of the twin towers. It's on the news all day long, which makes the day pass slowly and feel quiet. Tuesday is my busiest day, because I have the most classes. Nate picked me up because Dad is still trying to fix my truck. I really love that truck. My dad hates it but he still spends time working on it anyway. Nate is dating this girl called Bridget and I am not sure how I feel about her. She is super outgoing (sometimes not in a good way) and Nate is very placid. It's like putting electricity and water together and knowing it will start a fire. Still, I am nice to Bridget because Nate likes her and I don't want to start any arguments. Although sometimes she makes odd comments about why Nate comes over to my house and that he should always be at her house and not at mine. I think she thinks that I'm going to steal Nate from her, even though I have explained to her repeatedly that Nate is just my best friend. She even saw me make out with this girl at a party once (it was more like a quick kiss because I'm too shy) and yet she still seems unconvinced. Nate says not to worry about it, but

I do, because girlfriends can come between best friends. I've seen it before and it happens on nearly every episode of *Friday Night Lights*.

Nate is the goalie for our college lacrosse team. The season will start up again soon and the games are every Friday night. Most of our college follows the team and so does our town. Nate graduates this year just like me. I think he's hoping he will be drafted for a Major-League Lacrosse team. I never followed lacrosse before I met Nate, but now I know all the rules and the names of all his teammates. There's only a couple of guys I don't like because I think they're jerks, but Nate says that's okay because he thinks they're jerks, too. His team gets lots of outside attention and plays against major colleges across the country. Last year they were undefeated for the entire season. There was an article about it in The New York Times and everything. Nate's dad doesn't think lacrosse is a career and wants him to be an accountant, so they don't get along very well. Nate and I often talk about how his dad and my mom want us to grow up and become the people that they want us to be, not the people that *we* want to be. We have that in common. I hope Nate gets spotted by a scout because he is a good player. Our favorite team is the New York Lizards, and during the season, Nate and I go to some of their games. Once we road tripped out to North Carolina to watch them play the Charlotte Hounds. I'll never forget that weekend because it's the weekend I first told Nate why I was so sad all the time. He said that I had a right to be sad and that if some days were too much, we could get away, just the two of us. Nate is a really good friend, and I'm glad I have him.

Almost halfway through my sophomore year of college, I nearly dropped out. After the incident in October, things were so messy, I had to take some time off before the Christmas break. I was hospitalized for a couple days as well. If it weren't for my oceanography professor, I don't think I would have made it to my third year. Professor Martin is a great lady. This is the third year I've been in her class (she teaches different subjects). This semester, she's teaching Oceanography 501. She was also the person who first told me about the marine program in California. She said as long as I kept my grades up, I could apply in my fourth year. You have to fill out an application, submit a portfolio of your work experiences with marine animals, and also write a ten-page paper. If I get into the program, I need move to California, but I will be working for one of the biggest marine conservation hospitals in the United States. From there, I can go into any branch of marine research I want to. It's something that I want, but when you want something, chances are a lot of other people want it too.

Anyway, I have a lot of reading to do before bed. My four subjects this semester are: Oceanography 501, tropical ecology, aquatic botany, and marine mammalogy. Sometimes I'll ask my dad if he thinks the degradation of seaweed is a thing and he looks at me as if I've spoken in a different language. I should do these readings, talk soon.

Thanks for listening,
Kayden

September 19, 2012

Dear Keeper,

I'm sorry I haven't written in a while, I've been busy. But also, sometimes when things get bad I don't want to talk about it. I know it's silly of me because the whole reason I'm writing to you is to talk about the bad things and to share them with you. I am going to try harder, honest.

In the summer before I started college, my dad got me a job at the East Point Marine Life Center. I think he thought that because I wanted to study marine biology, it would look good to graduate having worked at the Center throughout college. It was just like my dad to think about my future while I was drowning in ways to escape it. The Center rescues marine animals, rehabilitates them, and then tries to release them back into the wild. If the animal can't be released for whatever reason, we give them a new home at the Center. Kip owns East Point Marina and has worked at the Marine Center for over thirty years. He also owns half of the Center, but he doesn't act like the owner. These days he plays a handful of roles: general manager, dive supervisor, tour guide, things like that. When I first met Kip, he was supposed to be training me for the job, but he didn't say a single word to me for eight days. Every time I tried to start a conversation with him he would just grunt at me. I didn't take this very well, mainly because I had only just moved into town and my one friend was my dad. It's not that I wanted Kip to be my friend, because at the time I didn't have anything in common with a sixty-something-year-old man, but I did want someone to talk to. I wanted to forget where I had just come from. I had been holding up well, but I felt empty at the same time, and I needed things to fill the emptiness.

The first thing he said to me was, "Pass the broom." That was on the eighth day. The second thing he said to me was, "You can have half my sandwich if you want." That was on the tenth day. Then on the thirteenth day, while we were cleaning the Ray Bay exhibit, he suddenly stopped cleaning the outside of the glass. Kip also told me to stop and listen. I hadn't been paying attention at first because I was busy trying to scrub a little black mark off the glass.

Then Kip said louder and more clearly, "You feel it?"

And I said something like, "Feel what?"

He replied, "It."

I looked at him for a while, and then instead of looking at him, I looked at the rays. Their wings cut through the water the way moments cut through time.

Then I said, which I will never forget, "Peace."

When I said that, I think something changed between Kip and I, because he told me that while she was alive, his daughter had loved manta rays and stingrays and she wanted to help with researching them. I had told him that she was at peace, too. It was strange to hear myself talking so calmly about death, but I felt like I had to for some reason.

Kip and I grew close after that day. I got my nickname from him the day after.

"Rayden," he calls me, after the rays. No one else calls me Rayden. It doesn't sound right unless Kip says it.

Ray Bay is our largest attraction. We have one fully grown reef manta ray and more than a dozen different species of stingrays. Manta rays are so big that it's not common to keep them in captivity, but ours was so badly injured that releasing her back into the wild would have been dangerous and she wouldn't have lived long. She's very special, but I will tell you about her soon. The Marine Center is split in half. One side is for the public, the other side is for rehabilitation and research. I am an Aquarist, which sounds neat, but most of what I do is exhibit cleaning, filter maintenance, food preparation (sometimes puke-worthy), and animal observation (my favorite, I'm always in Ray Bay). Sometimes I also help Kip and the other caretakers with breeding programs, and occasionally I sit in on vet procedures or assist if the resident nurse is away. Other times I shadow caretakers and help with mammal training. Although mostly I answer a lot of questions from children asking if sharks can break the glass or from teenagers asking if "Nemo wants to go home". On an average day, I am feeding the animals and cleaning up a lot. Do you know what starfish poop looks like? Trust me, I wish they pooped glitter.

Before college orientation day my freshman year, I almost decided not to go. I had only lived in East Point for a couple of months and had spent all my time at the Marine Center trying to figure out the job and not screw anything up. I was so scared of doing anything else that I used to cry in the staff room when I thought no one was listening, but Kip was. One afternoon, he asked me what was wrong. Back then I couldn't even ask someone what the time was, let alone share what I was feeling, so I just said nothing. I've never asked him why he didn't just leave the staff room that afternoon, but I am glad he didn't. He told me life outside the Marine Center isn't as scary as I thought it was. He said he had spoken with my dad and knew what I had come from, and that he was sure I would be okay. I think I asked him how he knew, and he said it's because some people in this world are like marine life: sometimes they just need someone to try extra hard to understand them. Before Kip, I had always wondered if anyone other than my therapist would understand the language I was speaking.

I forgot to mention that sometimes when we are super busy at the Center, I'm on photo duty. Basically, I have to greet the visitors and wait while they get themselves organized in front of a huge green screen, and I say things like, "Watch out! The shark is coming!" and they have to pull these surprised faces. Sharks don't usually act like that around people, but I have to pretend. Most days I am always pretending anyway. Except in Ray Bay.

Manta rays look like sharks that have been run over by bulldozers, but they are actually fish. They have the largest brain to body mass ratio of any fish. This means they are able to retain memory and can problem solve. I think this might be why Mahala remembers me. In those first few months, I just did my job. It wasn't until I interacted with Mahala for the first time that I really started to love these animals. I had come into Ray Bay ready to close up and she was low on the floor bed. At first, I panicked and thought something was wrong, but after a while, I noticed she was looking at me. I thought maybe she was hungry, but there was food in the tank. So I sat with her. She didn't move for an hour, she just watched me. Mahala was rescued off the coast of Florida. She was badly tangled in fishing wire and she's missing an eye. She has a thirteen-foot-long wingspan and is estimated to be about forty-five years old. They moved her into our Center five years ago. Mahala is easily one of the best parts of my week. She also loves lettuce. I mean she *loves* lettuce. It's a bit of a problem. We spend extra on lettuce just for her. Sometimes I will even pick some up on my way to work so she can have an extra treat. She's not my pet or anything and I know that, but it's hard not to love her. Part of me thinks she's what's kept me alive all these years, and I'm not sure what I would do without her.

It's hard to believe I have worked here for more than four years. Sometimes I wonder where I would be if I didn't work here. I usually work a full day on Wednesdays because I don't have class. Today, Kip and I spent most of the time in the back rooms with the coral reef exhibit. We have a thirty-meter tank with twenty thousand gallons of water that mimics natural reef ecosystems. We have both hard and soft corals and gorgonians. Many of our species are collected by Kip or other senior marine biologists to study here at the Center. Some species either can't survive in changing water temperatures or are endangered by overfishing, so they are here under our protection. This afternoon, someone spilled chocolate milkshake on the glass and it had dried and crusted. It was super annoying to clean because it had dripped everywhere. I don't mind the reef exhibit because it's very colorful and we have angelfish and sea cucumbers and crabs and they sometimes do very weird things which make me laugh.

Kip said to me while we were cleaning, "You lost in your head again?"

"Little."

"Seeing your therapist?"

"Yes."

"Good girl."

"Kip," I asked, "Would you miss me if I were gone?"

"Yes."

I have been thinking about this all night. Do you think more people would survive if someone told them they would be missed?

Thanks for listening,
Kayden

September 21, 2012

Dear Keeper,

Honestly, I love pumpkin spice lattes. Especially in the fall. I saw a commercial for them earlier, so I went and got one. I lost to marketing, but I don't care. I was supposed to go to Nate's game tonight, but I didn't want to leave the house. My dad is on a date. He hasn't been on a date for years and I don't even know how it happened. He came home this afternoon and told me he had serviced this woman's car and she asked him out to dinner. I've wanted my dad to start dating again because I don't want him to be alone, but it's weird at the same time. Meanwhile, I'm home alone with my latte hoping my dad is warm because I didn't see him leave the house with his coat and the weather is getting cooler.

East Point is filled with maple trees. I don't know whose idea it was to plant so many, but I don't mind because they look so pretty this time of year. Bright orange and yellow leaves line the sidewalks and you can see the colors for miles. It's very different from my old town. I was born in Edmonson, Colorado, a small town surrounded by mountains. In the summer the mountains are very beautiful, but in winter the days are cold and it snows a lot. Edmonson's population is pretty small, and, like all small towns, most people know each other's business like it's their own. My dad has always told me that he had only meant to be passing through. He'd taken a gap year before college and was on his way to a football game in California. This was until he saw my mom. I'm not sure if it was love at first sight because neither of them talk about how they first fell in love. It's hard to talk about things like that when you are divorced. My dad ended up staying in Edmonson, marrying my mom, and opening an auto shop. Edmonson is a very religious town. Most people that live there have very traditional views. My dad originally grew up in Long Island (not East Point, he lived closer to the city) and he wasn't much into God. He still went to church and listened to my mom talk about the

Bible a lot, but he never had an opinion on it and we don't talk about religion much.

"Causes too many arguments," he once said. "Don't talk about religion or politics at a dinner table, Kayden."

Which I never would anyway because I don't get invited to many dinner tables.

My mom however *is* religious. People in Edmonson called her a Southern belle. She is beautiful with long blonde hair and bright blue eyes. She is like a summer's day after the winter has been incredibly raw. My mother also does not believe in homosexuality. This makes things with her and I, well, a little complicated. Actually, it makes things very complicated, but I think you get the point. My mother is a good woman. She is the committee organizer for her church. I am going to call it "The Church of Grace" because I don't want you to get upset or anything and try to find this church. I also don't want you thinking it's not a good church, because it is, it's just that they have different ideas about things. But not everyone in Edmonson has the same views as my mother. In fact, Mr. Whittertaker, who lived next door to us while I was growing up, said to me once that it didn't matter who I loved because God would love me anyway. This is a nice thought, and I hope it's true.

I didn't have very many friends in high school. You probably think that this is what it's like for everyone, but it wasn't like that for my mom when she was in high school. She was popular and became Student Body President in her senior year. I think she had hoped that her daughter would be the same, but everybody at my school thought I was weird and too quiet. They didn't like my hair or my freckles or the way I wore my clothes and so they teased me about it. Relentlessly. After a while you get used to people making fun of you. It didn't matter that I went to the same church, sang the same hymns, and attended all the same classes. The people at my school knew I was different and they punished me for it. The strangest thing was that, for a long time, I punished myself for it, too.

My parents both handled the fact that I liked women very differently. Dad was quiet, but he told me that he loved me and he just wanted me to be happy. Mom, however, acted like the world had ended for her. She also believed I was ruining her image. She figured I had plotted the entire thing to embarrass her. She asked if I needed more allowance, if I was rebelling because she and Dad hadn't bought me a car. At one point, she even asked if I wanted to stop going to church. She said if I was bored, that I didn't have to go, I just had to stop being gay. I think she was desperate back then. I know she still has hope these days, but it's a quiet hope, the type of hope she doesn't dare bring up or else I'll hang up the phone and not speak to her for months. Back then, she made me read the Bible a lot, too. She told me that she had been to many pastors and they advised her that reading the Bible would set me on the right path again. She dragged me to church camps and conversion therapy sessions. She pleaded, begged, cried, and ignored me once for three weeks. But none of this changed the way I felt.

Don't get me wrong, after all this I still consider myself

lucky. Which sounds like a funny way to put it because it was an ordeal when it didn't need to be. It's just, some people don't survive the torture they are subjected to. I knew someone who didn't survive, and I loved her. At the time, even in all the confusion and all the misery, I had this beacon of light. But then the light went out, and I have not been the same since.

Thanks for listening,
Kayden

September 24, 2012

Dear Keeper,

People leave things in our campus library all the time. They leave scarves in winter, water bottles in summer, they leave jackets and car keys and once someone even left their retainer. These things can all be taken to lost property and recovered. But today I left my feelings in the library. I hadn't meant to. I was in a rush this morning when I left for school, so I forgot to bring this notebook to write in. While I was in the library I suddenly had this urge to share, so I stupidly decided to write on a piece of paper, and then I accidentally left the paper - along with my aquatic botany textbook - behind. When I realized, I was halfway through the mac and cheese Dad had made for dinner. He doesn't make the best mac and cheese, but I eat it because he thinks he does. Dad looked at me and asked what was wrong and I just said it had been a hard day. Every time I tell him I've had a hard day, he asks when my next therapy session is. As though a hard day is enough to tip me over the edge. I wish he would just understand, but he doesn't.

I cried because I didn't want anyone to read what I had written. I'm not ready to share things with anybody. Someday yes, but not yet. I wish I had never written anything down and just kept it inside until I had come home to you. I feel stupid and embarrassed and I just want to crawl up in bed and never think about anything again. The thoughts are bad tonight. At dinner, I knew my dad could tell because he suggested we watch a movie together. He only ever watches movies with me when things are bad. I told Dad I just wanted to sit in my room. I've been sitting here listening to my radio for over an hour and I can't sleep. I never used to be like this. I know you probably think I have always been like this, but it's not true. There was a time when I wasn't always so anxious and sad. There is a lot to tell you, and I feel like crying again because it hurts to talk about this. But I am going to try and write it all down.

Falling in love makes you feel weightless. In high school, I met a girl who made me feel like the whole sky. Her name was Shaye. The first time I saw Shaye was at the start of junior year. She was sitting in my English class and I didn't know who she was because she was new. I was also annoyed because she had sat in my seat and everyone knew that it was *my* seat. I didn't ask her to move or anything because I couldn't imagine being the new person at school and then having some person tell you to move out of their seat. So instead I sat in the seat behind her. I remember thinking she smelled nice. Her hair was long and her skin looked soft and her school skirt was above the knee, not below. She turned around to me at one point and asked if I had a spare pen. I think I would have given her a spare kidney if she needed it because the way she asked and the way she smiled made everything in my stomach feel light.

Shaye was also in another four of my classes. The first time we had an entire conversation was in our science class because the teacher said she had to be my lab partner. I can't remember what we were supposed to be doing. I think we were dissecting frog legs. But during the lesson, I accidentally flicked the scalpel and the flesh flew sideways and landed in another girl's hair. Shaye and I looked at each other and tried not to laugh for the rest of the class. It didn't take long after that day to want to be around her whenever I could. We liked the same music and I liked the way she dressed. She had made friends with some older people in college and they would drive us to gigs and sneak us in even though we didn't have fake IDs or anything. Shaye was crazy and vibrant and reckless, but she did it in a way that seemed cool to me. She was the first person who told me that even if the world seemed scary, it was scarier to hide from it. But Shaye was also sad.

Her parents worked a lot, so she drank a lot and she did more drugs than I had ever seen or heard of in my entire life. It was like she had become so damaged that she didn't know how else to be. The first time I kissed her I felt the poison as it rolled down the back of my throat. I was only sixteen. I knew things were changing, and I knew we were more than friends, but I didn't know what to call it. Shaye didn't want to call it anything. She said she wanted me, but she didn't want anyone else to know we were together. In the beginning, I was fine with that. It was just like having a best friend, only we'd make out for hours and have sex when her parents weren't home. Her parents were nice people, but they were oblivious. They seemed like open people so I didn't understand why we couldn't tell them about us, but Shaye told me that I didn't know them like she did. After a while, the high didn't feel the way it was supposed to. I begged Shaye to let me tell my parents we were together. I thought if my parents knew then it would be real between us. In the summer before we started senior year, she finally gave in and said we could come out to my parents. I was stupid to think that my love for Shaye was the only thing in the world, because it wasn't. People's opinions still existed.

Telling my parents made things worse. Even though I think my mom already knew, sometimes when we don't say things, they aren't real. When it became real to her, she tried to pretend it wasn't. My mom didn't want me to ever see Shaye again, and my dad told her she was being ridiculous. This only made them fight more. I think the day I came out was the day I died to her. Suddenly all the things she expected me to be and all the things she thought I would have weren't going to happen. She would never have a son-in-law, she would never see her daughter walk down the aisle to marry a man, and she would never find herself in the waiting room at the hospital holding her son-in-law's hand while her daughter gave birth to her grandchild. For all these things my mother wanted, she never once stopped to ask what it was that *I* wanted. It wasn't like I was asking *her* to like women, I was just telling her that *I* liked them. Maybe that's why it became so hard to talk about anything else I liked because I was afraid she would get mad at me for liking those things, too. I'm not sure my mother knew how much pain she caused me. It's something that we don't speak about. I still struggle to talk to her sometimes when she calls.

She's difficult to talk to without the giant elephant listening in on the phone conversation. Every time she said I needed to "change back" like I could easily undo who I was, or every time she referred to me as being wrong, or the time she said that she didn't deserve this, I wondered if she ever stopped and thought about how much her words hurt me. Her own daughter. The child she had brought into the world, who she had vowed to love and care for. Instead in those years, it felt like we were at war. It was hard not having my mom to confide in.

I wanted to tell her that I love women, I love everything about them. I love the way they move, the way they look, speak, act. I love the way they smell and the different shapes and sizes they can be. But it was this love that caused such distress and hatred from my mother, and that's something I'll never quite understand. After the reaction from my mom, Shaye became even more petrified to tell anyone else. So we went back to hiding things, which worked for a little while. Until a couple of weeks into our senior year, Ben Clark, a boy in our class, caught us kissing behind the bleachers one afternoon. He told everyone. He said we were lesbians and he labeled us before either of us had the chance to figure it all out properly ourselves. Things didn't go so well after that. Shaye and I argued a lot. People were mean. They were so mean that some nights I used to cry myself to sleep. I try not to blame the students who taunted us. I don't think it was their fault. I think that they just didn't understand and I think that their parents would tell them mean things. One week a speaker came to our school to talk about college applications to the seniors. Parents were invited as well. I remember this clearly because Shaye's mom and my mom exchanged glances before making us sit on opposite sides of the gymnasium. While I was trying to make eye contact with Shaye through the crowd, I overheard Cally Andrews' dad say; "Stay away from that Kayden girl, she will give you homosexuality." I still remember the way Cally snickered. Mr Andrews is a beefy looking man and ran Bible study on Saturdays for the elementary school across town. I don't think he'd ever known a lesbian before me.

Maybe it was my radio that kept me going, because Shaye became even sadder. She became even more damaged and I didn't think that was possible. Then everything changed in October, seven months before we were meant to graduate high school. It was a Thursday when I found out. You never forget when you hear something like that. Not ever, even if you want to. You remember every detail. What day it was, the time, what you were wearing, what you had eaten that day, and what you couldn't eat for the rest of the day. You remember exactly what you were doing on a day when everything changes. It was 4:15 in the afternoon, and I was alone in my bedroom. I had been reading *A Farewell to Arms* by Ernest Hemingway for school. I haven't read this book since. I left it at my mom's house when I moved. If I think about Frederic and Catherine, I see Shaye's face and I feel sick. My dad had walked into my bedroom and he looked like he had something to say but he didn't want to say it at the same time. He looked sad, but sad in a way that he was sad for me. He told me he loved me and that he was sorry. I don't know why I thought of Shaye when he said that, but I did. She hadn't answered my texts all morning.

Shaye had killed herself.

Then I had asked how, and he said she had hurt herself and her brother had found her. The first thing I had thought was that maybe I should have called her instead. In the days afterwards, I couldn't concentrate on anything. I thought Shaye's death was my fault. Like I hadn't paid enough attention to her or that she felt like I didn't love her. I did love her. She was the first person I think I ever loved. After she died, I tried to understand how life could go on because I was so sure that mine had stopped. They never taught that in our school, how life goes on even after something bad happens. I wish my teachers had taught me that some questions can never be answered. I wish they had taught me how to forgive myself.

Shaye's parents held her funeral a month after her death because the police had still been investigating. The funeral hurt a lot. It was also strange. They had this photo of her in the church and she was smiling and she looked like the happiest girl in the world. It was such a lie but she still looked so beautiful. Sadness isn't meant to be beautiful and I don't understand why I thought hers was. Her dad didn't say a single word throughout the ceremony. He sat in the pews staring at the coffin and he didn't look away once. Her brother cried and her sister wasn't there and her mom had a breakdown as they were taking the coffin away. She screamed and she cried and she was yelling, "How could you do this to us?" and I have never forgotten those words, ever. There were people there that Shaye had never told me about. She had aunts and cousins and people from her old city who came all the way here for her funeral. It made me realize that maybe I didn't know everything about Shaye like I thought I had. This made me feel out of place.

But I wanted to say goodbye, too. Students from school were there as well. Even the mean ones. This made me mad because I knew they were only there because they had to be. I didn't know if I was crying because I was sad or angry.

We had a separate assembly for Shaye at school a week after her funeral. I cried a lot during that, too. I was still so angry because they didn't know what her favorite color was or where she liked to be kissed or about the teddy bear shirt she wore to bed. They had been so mean to us, how could they just stand around and feel sorry for her when they had been so mean to her before? Everything at school changed after Shaye died. People who had never spoken to me came up to me at lunch and told me they were sorry she was gone. They asked me how I was, if I needed anything, if I wanted to talk, and told me they would be there for me.

"My grandmother died, Kayden. I know what you are going through."

"Sorry she killed herself, Kayden. We are here for you."

"It must be so hard, you can talk to me."

Other people weren't nice at all. They said horrible things like how Satan had called her back and she deserved to die. All the teachers treated me differently. I never got detention again and they always asked me how I was. The student counselor always seemed to be walking the same way I was to my next class. No one was mad if I forgot to do homework and they gave me extra time for papers and exams even though I didn't need it. Honestly, I think they probably thought I was going to kill myself too. A month after her funeral was December. Edmonson was always so pretty around Christmas time. All over town, lights were strung up and trees were decorated and it would snow. I should have been happy over the holidays, but all I could feel was sadness. I remember it was a Sunday night, two days before Christmas, and Dad had finally agreed to let me drive his car. I liked the quiet of the streets in the late evening, they helped calm my thoughts. But then Shaye's favorite song came on the radio for the first time since she had died. That was the only time I had ever thought about killing myself. The road was stretched before me, the night was dark, but the stars were out. I thought to myself, this wouldn't be a bad way to die. It was just the open road with her song on the radio and my head filled with thoughts of Shaye. I thought about running my car into one of the telephone poles along the highway, tall silhouettes heading to somewhere that had to be better than here. I never drove my car into them, though. I drove home instead and cried. I didn't stop crying for a long time.

I missed her every hour when she had gone. I mean I always knew that I would miss her if we broke up or moved away from each other, but this was a different kind of missing her. It was a type of sadness I'd never felt before. It just seemed to fill every part of me. I would walk around the school to find her, even though I knew I wouldn't. I saw her in things all the time, like blueberry muffins because those were her favorite and the bottom of whiskey bottles because we used to sneak them from her dad's liquor cabinet. I almost drank myself into oblivion one night. In the new year, I found myself starting to laugh again and then I'd cry because I knew I couldn't show her what had made me laugh and then I'd feel guilty for being a tiny bit happy because I felt like I should be sad forever without her. I'd want to hear her voice all the time. I lost count of the amount of times I called her voicemail or texted her, and then suddenly one day I called and an automated message came back saying the number had been disconnected. It felt like losing her all over again.

Then Shaye's parents moved away. The "For Sale" sign was put on their front lawn three months after her funeral. I remember because it was a week before my eighteenth birthday. They had buried her in Edmonson but I guess the town had become too hard to be in. I asked my dad if he thought they would be able to start again in a new town, and why were they leaving Shaye behind, but he said parents carry their children wherever they go. I still think about that now, if something ever happened to me if my dad would still know where to find me.

All my life I've known my parents to fight, but after Shaye died and the whole town found out I was gay, they started to fight all the time. They had been having problems for a while, but this seemed to really cause a rift. They didn't make a point to hide it, either. My dad talked to me a lot about how things weren't working. You never expect to be your parent's shoulder; you always expect it to be the other way around. Somehow all the grief and hurt I was holding inside because of Shaye was put aside and I had to be a mediator for my parents. My mom stopped talking to me after a while. She stopped telling me that she loved me and she blamed a lot of things on me. She got angry with me for so many things and I never understood why. But my dad understood me in ways my mom never did, and it's still like that now. I don't have any brothers or sisters. My mom once said it was because when I was born, her and Dad didn't know how they could possibly share the love they had for me with anyone else. I wanted to know where this love went when I needed it from her the most, but I never told her that. My mom never told my dad about the conversion therapy sessions either. But when he found out, he told her that he would drop me off and pick me up each day. At this point he didn't seem to love my mom anymore, and he never took me to the sessions again. Instead he took me to his auto shop and I would spend my afternoons there. The shop had these old marine biology magazines in the office. I spent every afternoon reading them from cover to cover. We didn't have a beach near Edmonson, the nearest is over fourteen hours away. I think this is where my love for the ocean started. I had lost Shaye and I still loved her even though I could never have her again, but I had found the ocean, which was something I could get to if I found a way. I had also always been good at science in high school, so I told my teacher about it and he said there were lots of colleges that offered courses in marine science. I didn't know what college I was going to apply for, I just knew I wanted to study marine biology.

When the pastor told my mom that I hadn't been going to therapy, she bugged out. She went crazy one night and threw my grandma's china set across the kitchen and it missed my dad by inches. That was it. I could see whatever sympathy and care my dad had left for my mother vanish. He sold the auto shop in Edmonson, filed for divorce, and told me he was moving to East Point, Long Island to open a new auto shop. He wanted me to come with him, but I couldn't because I still had two months left to graduate high school. That's when I decided I wanted to apply for a college in East Point. I applied one night after a big fight with my mom. She had tried everything she possibly could to undo my sexuality, and it still didn't work. So then she decided to act like I wasn't in the house. Those last two months in Edmonson were bad. People would stop my mother in the street and offer their condolences. They looked at her as if I had died, and nearly always I was standing right beside her. When you are eighteen and the entire town thinks there is something wrong with you, it makes you think very dark things. I got a fake ID, I drank a lot, and I slept with a few girls. I met them at bars and parties that I shouldn't have been going to. I was not in a good place. I didn't have feelings for these girls and I almost always woke up crying. I don't know why I did that, I think I just wanted to feel something. Shaye's death had left me so empty, and when you don't think you will ever feel again, even pain and sadness is comforting to you. I don't even know how I graduated high school in early June. It still seems like I was someone else in that time. I also got my letter saying I had been accepted into college. I called up my dad and I was so happy. He said he would get a job for me as well. At that point I wanted to do anything that would get me away from my mom. I moved at the beginning of summer. The last thing my mom said to me before I left was, "Don't go."

Those words have haunted me ever since.

Back then, I thought I was leaving all the sadness behind and it almost made me happy. It turns out sadness can't be left in places. At least not when it's stitched so deeply under your skin. I am not ashamed of who I am, and I don't regret coming out. But some nights when I can't sleep, all I can think about is that if I had never said anything at all, maybe my parents would still be married and Shaye would be alive.

It's late and I'm sorry I wrote so much tonight. I have a test in the morning and I haven't studied. I don't think it counts towards anything, but I hate when I don't know things.

Thanks for listening,
Kayden

September 25, 2012

Dear Keeper,

Someone wrote back to my letter. The first thing I did when I got to campus today was to go to the library. My textbook was still sitting on the desk. Inside, there was my letter, but also another note along with it. Obviously, I opened it, and I'll tell you what it said.

I used to pretend I was fine when I wasn't, too. I thought there was a cure for sadness, but I think it always stays with you. If you want to share your secrets with me, you can write back. Leave the note in your textbook and put it in the left shelf, second row. I'll find it.

At first, I was wondering if this person was just another student wanting free access to my aquatic botany textbook, which is very expensive, but they sounded honest. Today was a hard day because Nate wasn't at school. We were meant to study together after my classes, but he'd had a fight with Bridget and didn't wait for me. So instead I chose to study alone. Most days I don't mind being alone, but it gets hard around this time of year. Shaye's anniversary will be in a couple of weeks.

Before I was born, my mom thought I was going to be a boy. That's why my parents picked Kayden. Then when I did arrive and I turned out to be a girl, my dad didn't want to change my name. My mom started calling me Kay when I came out as gay; she said it made me sound more feminine. In that summer before the whole school and town found out, she tried desperately to convince me I was just going through a phrase. One night she'd had too many glasses of wine and she said she hoped that if I was reminded I was a girl, it would make me like boys again. I wish I didn't have to say anything at all, that being gay was the same as me being straight. My mother thought I wasn't the same person. Like someone else had taken over and I had been replaced. But I was still me. If she had asked me, *which she never did*, I would have said it was the opposite. It felt like the person who had been there all along was finally breathing. Like I was finally alive.

In the years following my "change" as she still calls it, there were times where I thought coming out wasn't worth it. I used to think that things would never get better. I remember the first conversation we had after I moved to East Point. It started with how the town was, how college was, and what the weather was like. And then she said, "You can overcome your homosexuality, Kayden," which made me feel like I had some type of disease.

"You can be cured," she said when I didn't answer. "This sin is not unforgivable, we can get you back to normal."

She continued to say things like that, until one day I just stopped answering her calls. I just hated that word, "normal". Why does my mother get to choose what is normal and what isn't? *That* doesn't seem normal.

I have said this to my therapist many times, but I will tell you, too. I am afraid to love someone again. It's not because I don't know how to love someone, but because I think my love killed Shaye. I loved her so much and I told her that the world should know this, even if she didn't want it to. I promised her it would be okay. But it wasn't okay. My own mother told me that my feelings were wrong. But I loved Shaye anyway, even when she told me that we should go back to hiding it. I loved her even when she told me that she couldn't handle what people were saying. I loved her and she killed herself because of it.

My therapist has been talking about sharing so much lately that I'm going to write back to the letter. You know, maybe I'll even make a new friend.

Thanks for listening,
Kayden

September 26, 2012

Dear Keeper,

My professor for tropical ecology has already handed out our first paper. My dad also burned dinner last night and the smell is still in our kitchen. Sometimes I study in my room, other times in the kitchen, and when I can't study in my house, I am in the campus library. Only today I can't study because the person already wrote back to my letter. I keep thinking I might catch them in the act. I imagine scenarios where I meet them in person and maybe the look on their face is sad and maybe it isn't. Of course, if I did see someone leaving a letter, I would probably freeze or hide. It's easier to share my feelings when I'm writing the words down. When I try to say the words out loud they come out wrong. But on paper, they sound right. In the letter, the person mentioned Sleepy Ears will be playing at our campus bar in a couple of weeks. This is not a very well-known band, it's just some college students who like music a lot and created a band in between their chemistry classes, or so I read on their YouTube channel. I was impressed the person in my letters knew who they were. I wrote a long letter and I told them about my radio. This sounds strange, but when I am writing to them, it feels the same as writing to you. I am wondering if this is what it feels like to share yourself with others.

Thanks for listening,
Kayden

September 28, 2012

Dear Keeper,

I never told you how my dad's date went. He said it was a disaster. The woman asked him strange questions like if he wore odd socks. I told him maybe she'd had bad experiences with men who wore odd socks, and he looked at me as though he didn't know if I was trying to be funny. Then he said, "Do you get your weirdness from me or your mother?"

I said him, but he said my mom, and that made us laugh. I didn't have work today, so I walked to Dad's shop. It is a long walk, but the weather was pretty, so I didn't mind. The leaves crunching under my feet sounded like someone eating a bowl of Cheerios, and I was hungry by the time I got there. Dad had also finally fixed my truck. He laughed with the other mechanics and made jokes about how much stress the truck caused him, but when he handed me the keys he whispered in my ear that he'd always fix this truck for me. My dad is sweet like that, he always wants to make me happy. I try to smile as much as I can around him, because I know that makes him worry less. Sometimes it's hard to smile, though. I had only just turned on the engine when Nate texted me and said he had forgotten his textbook at my house. He is always leaving things at my house which makes Bridget very angry (I don't know why she is so insane), so I told him I would bring it to campus with me.

When I got to campus and gave him his textbook, he said he was in a rush because he was late for class. He asked me to wait until his class was over and he'd meet me again. I wasn't sure if I was going to go to his game tonight, so I said I would wait so we could hang out. Sometimes I don't feel like going to Nate's games. I feel bad about it. Our other friends Joe and Tyler always go to every single game, even if it's raining. But sometimes I can't be around people. It's not that I don't want to be, it just makes me anxious. I hope one day it won't be as hard.

I went to the library to wait for Nate. I like the campus library because it's usually very quiet. There are students concentrating, not like the public library in town. In the public library, the librarian is always telling people to be quiet. I suggested once to put up a "be quiet" sign, and she gave me such a stern look that I never went back there again. Our college library is in the middle of campus. There are two sections: upstairs and downstairs. The ceilings are very high, and they have big lights hanging from them, like chandeliers only they aren't made with diamonds or anything like that. There are lots of columns stretching up from the floor and they have patterns carved in them. The columns separate each aisle of books. The floor is tiled like a hallway but then each aisle has carpet where the book shelves sit. The carpet is so ugly. I don't know why they chose the ugliest carpet but I suppose people don't come here to stare at the carpet. There is a desk in the very far corner between the marine science aisle and chemistry aisle. Usually it's empty because the vent above it is broken and it lets in cold air in the winter and drips water in the summer. I always sit at this desk because no one is ever here. When I got to the desk today, I almost didn't see my aquatic botany textbook because it had been pushed so far back into the shelf. After panicking that it had been stolen, I managed to drag it out, and I opened the book to find another note. I got butterflies because I had only just replied to the previous letter the other day. When I opened it, the letter said, "Maybe I will see you at Sleepy Ears. Wear white if you want to meet up."

Honestly, I even looked around. It was stupid, I am ashamed to admit that I did it, but I thought maybe the letter had been left recently and I could catch who was leaving them. Obviously, I wouldn't know, because I don't know what the person looks like. Also "wear white" is not helpful. Everybody wears white shirts. And I only have one white shirt because my skin is fair, and if I wear white, I sort of blend in with the cotton. Anyway, I stayed in the library and waited for Nate and I wrote back. At the end of the letter, I said, *My name is Kayden, what's yours?*

Thanks for listening,
Kayden

October 6, 2012

Dear Keeper,

I am trying, but things are hard. Today I had a scheduled shift at the Marine Center, but Kip called me and said that they didn't need me to come in. The actual floor manager is Don. He's a friend of my dad's, which is why I started working here without so much as an interview. He's truly a nice man and has a lot of experience with marine life. He was a professional surfer when he was younger. While competing in Hawaii, he was attacked by a 12-foot-long tiger shark. The shark tore three of his major ligaments, and he was forced to quit surfing. He has a giant scar on his leg and walks with a limp when it's cold out. Don likes to tell all the kids that come to the Center about his scar. He tells them that instead of hating sharks, he decided to help them.

We have five different species of sharks here at the Marine Center. Don says not enough people understand why sharks attack so they are afraid of them. He says that the ocean is the home of the shark, and when we enter, we must respect this. I have sat in on more daily shark talks than I can count. Although once halfway through Don's big speech about conserving all life, some kid threw up in the jellyfish pools and Kip was yelling at me over our walkie talkies, so I had to scramble to save them. What I am trying to share with you is that Don was attacked by a great big shark, and he is not afraid. But I think he is afraid of me.

When I got sick, my dad spoke to Don a lot. They're old friends, so I understand, but he's also my boss, which is weird. At one point, Don even sent me flowers while I was in the hospital. Don is not afraid of sharks because he believes that he understands them, but he is afraid of me because, well, he doesn't understand me. I think this is why he keeps away from me as much as possible. He probably assumes that if he orders me around I am going to hurt myself. When people find out that you have anxiety or you are depressed or you have been dealing with sadness for quite some time, they either avoid you, make fun of you, or act like each moment they are with you they are walking on eggshells. Don acts like the third. I think he feels like at any moment I might split open and all my sadness will fall out onto the floor and he is not going to know what to say. Then again, most people don't.

When Shaye died, everyone around me said that time would heal me. But with or without time, Shaye was still gone. I could no longer talk to her, hold her, or tell her about my day. This made me so sad that I started to get sick. I would think about very bad things, especially at night and when I was alone. During this time, I didn't want to kill myself, but I didn't want to be alive either. I just wanted the thoughts to be quiet. I wanted silence.

People notice when you are sad. Sometimes they only notice because they can't make you happy. For some reason this frustrates people. My mom noticed first. Then my dad, then all my friends and my teachers. This is why I followed my dad to East Point. It helped me. Nate made me smile again, my professors kept me motivated, and the Marine Center introduced me to things I never even knew existed.

It made me forget things. All of it distracted me, but I was still sad.

I'm ready to tell you about the incident that happened in my sophomore year of college. Before I write it down, I just want to say that I'll never do anything like it ever again. I hope you believe me. After it happened, I didn't tell anyone, but my dad still found out and it scared him. It scared him so much that he said I needed to go to the hospital. It's difficult because you can't take someone who is sad to the emergency room and stitch them up. I didn't have any external trauma, there was no immediate cure in the emergency room. There were only nurses and doctors to prescribe antidepressants or induce me if they thought I was going to harm myself. It was about three days after Shaye's anniversary. I'd been home alone in my room and received an email. The email was from Shaye's mom. I hadn't spoken to her since Shaye's funeral. I'm not going to go into detail about what the email said because I've tried to block out all the words. She blamed me. She said that before Shaye and I were together she was happier and didn't get caught up in horrible things. She said that Shaye wouldn't have killed herself if it hadn't been for me. I could tell you that this is what triggered everything. I could tell you that Shaye's mom brought out all the sadness and the grief I had been pushing down since moving to East Point. But it wasn't. It was Shaye, or at least the memory of her.

I went for a walk. And I remember slamming the front door as though I was angry with the world, which was strange because I don't remember feeling angry. I didn't concentrate on the direction I was going, I just kept walking. It must have been at least half an hour of walking before I thought I saw Shaye. To this day, I don't know if I believe in spirits and if that's what this was or if it was all in my head, but I followed her. I must have walked for over an hour because I ended up near the marina. There is a bridge that overlooks East Point not far from there. If you follow the bridge, you can keep going all the way out to the freeway.

East Point is an average sort of town. Our roads have potholes and most of the shop fronts need a paint job, but I still think it's pretty. It's the trees that make it look like an oil painting from up on the bridge. All these gray and brick buildings, but the trees line all the roads. I still drive up and park my truck near the bridge. I listen to my radio and things like that, especially when the thoughts in my head get to be too much.

But on that day, I was following someone I shouldn't have been. Shaye climbed over the railing and disappeared. I've tried to explain this part to my therapist but it's never made any sense. I climbed the railing too, and looking down, I wasn't thinking about ending my life. I was just thinking about following Shaye. A truck honking broke the trance I had been in and I stepped back off the railing. The truck had slowed down but the driver didn't get out. I remember feeling scared, so I ran. I ran all the way back home. The next week, my dad got a call from one of his suppliers. It had been his son driving the truck and he recognized me. Dad took me to the hospital that afternoon.

Of course, neither of us knew what to do when we got

there. It's not like you can say, "Hello, my daughter is still experiencing grief from high school, I am not sure if she wants to kill herself, but I was hoping maybe you would be able to tell?" So we sat in the emergency room in silence until one of the nurses asked what the issue was. My dad was flustered because he didn't know what to say. I didn't want him to be embarrassed, so I told the nurse I wanted to kill myself. You should have seen her face. Everyone in the room went very quiet and the nurses all looked at each other. Maybe it was because I had said it too calmly. But no one understood that the reason I was so calm was because I wasn't trying to kill myself, I didn't feel like I wanted to die. I was just sad because my girlfriend *had*.

Because I'd told the nurses I wanted to die, I had to be monitored for a minimum of seventy-two hours. The doctors diagnosed depression, and on paper, this made sense to me. But in my heart and in my mind, not so much. It's not that I didn't want to happy, it's not that I had forgotten how to be happy or that I couldn't be happy. It was that I wasn't sure if I was *allowed* to be happy. It is very easy to smile when you are sad. You smile because you don't want anyone to ask what is wrong. If they ask you, then there is a high chance you won't be able to stop yourself from crying. When I cry, my face goes red and my eyes get blotchy and I look like a total mess. I never want people to see me cry, ever. It's easier for me to smile at people and tell them I'm fine. People don't want to know about your problems, they only think they do. They're too busy with their own.

After the hospital stay, I came home and my dad googled

a lot. I think he was trying to find answers but didn't want to ask the questions out loud.

"You are fragile," he would say, "you need help."

I don't blame him, because I did need help and I knew that he was scared and I knew that he didn't know how to handle me. Things got really bad at school and at work. I would shut off for days at a time without saying a word. But I am not fragile. At least I didn't think I was, until everybody started saying it. Then I started to believe them.

Joe told me that Xanax helped him sleep, so he gave me some. I took it one night when I started to wonder if Shaye's "spirit" might come back to me. My dad caught me taking it and thought I was taking something worse. I couldn't convince him that everything was fine and so he insisted I go to group counseling sessions. They are held at the community center. They still send me a Christmas card each year. I met some nice people in those sessions, but I didn't go for very long. They said that the sessions were for people feeling the same things. I suppose we were all feeling the same things, but we handled them differently. So to me, it was strange that they grouped us all together like that. There was a girl in my group that had cuts all the way up her arms. She told me it was because it felt good, that she didn't feel the pain when she was doing it. I didn't tell her, but it looked very painful to me.

I met my therapist there, too. I hadn't meant to really, I thought she was a mom picking up her kid or something. At least that's the first impression I got of her. But then she handed me a business card, and she said to contact her if I wanted to talk.

Before she left she said, "Death hurts, Kayden."

I wanted to tell her that I knew that already, I could feel how much it hurt, but then she said, "What hurts even more than death is grief."

And I didn't know what to say back because I felt whatever had broken inside me, move.

Thanks for listening,
Kayden

October 9, 2012

Dear Keeper,

It's very late, or early, depending on how you look at it. It's 3am in the morning and I can't sleep. Yesterday after my classes, Nate was supposed to drop me off at home, but he started fighting with Bridget in the middle of the college parking lot. They yelled at each other over the phone for ages and it made me feel uncomfortable and then Nate yelled at me. Nate has never yelled at me before. I feel like I need my friends more than they think I need them. They are still going through their normal lives trying to figure their own things out and I am just here, still thinking about the bad things that happened years ago. I want to tell them that I am falling apart, especially Nate, but he has his own problems. There is this saying and it goes something like, "Be good to people because everyone is fighting their own battles." I know that Nate is having a hard time with Bridget, but I'm having a hard time with *everything*. What do you do when your battle is so great you can't think about anyone else's? I yelled back at Nate and told him that he didn't have to take it out on me and then he said I wasn't the only one with problems. I took the bus home and didn't talk to him for the rest of the day.

Then after dinner, when I went back to my room he texted me and said he was sorry.

I'm sorry Kayden, I was stupid. Bridget just makes me mad.

Well, why are you with her?

I'm scared to be alone.

A long time ago I asked my dad why he stayed with my mom for so long if he wasn't happy. He told me it was because sometimes life makes you sacrifice your own happiness for someone else's. I understand why my dad did this. There were times when I was not happy with Shaye, but I stayed because I loved her so much and I just wanted *her* to be happy. But in the end, I couldn't make her happy because I don't think you can undo someone in the same way they can undo themselves.

I wanted to tell Nate that he shouldn't be with Bridget if he is unhappy, but I am not exactly an expert on happiness. Instead I texted him back.

I understand.

Do you forgive me?

Yes.

Also, the person in my letters is named Alex. I hope we can be good friends, because I feel like I can tell him anything. Yesterday in my letter I asked him what he thinks it would take for someone to break and then come back again. I can't wait for him to reply.

Thanks for listening,
Kayden

October 11, 2012

Dear Keeper,

Today is Shaye's anniversary. It has been five years since she died. In our session this morning, my therapist asked, "Why do you still punish yourself, Kayden?"

It is easy for me to tell you that I blame myself for Shaye's death. What isn't easy is admitting that deep down, I know I wasn't the reason for it. When my therapist says it wasn't my fault, I understand. When my father held me as I stained his shirt with more tears than motor oil, I knew that I could not have stopped her, even if I tried. But in the moments when I am sad and the space around me feels like it is closing in, I am convinced that I should keep punishing myself. Because I asked her to share when she didn't want to. I forced her to come out when she wasn't ready. All because I thought it would make us stronger.

I haven't really told you the reason why Shaye and I would go to gigs. It was because the people there didn't judge us. We could never be ourselves in public, so it felt good to be able to hide away with other people that didn't care if we were together or not. When we first kissed, she told me that we could never tell anyone. She said that people in Edmonson would not accept us. When we went to gigs, she would kiss me all the time. Shaye used to get high and I used to watch her and wonder where her mind went. She said it was always on me, but there was something about the way she would look up into the sky. It was like she was searching for something out there, something she couldn't get here on Earth. One night we went to a gig three towns over. Afterwards, Shaye got us invited to a house party. I remember lots of older college people being there. Shaye started talking to this girl and the only thing I can remember about her is she had extremely long hair. She asked us where we were from and we said Edmonson. Then she said something like it must be hard being out and Shaye and I just sort of looked at each other but didn't say anything to her. She asked if we had heard of a boy called Josh (I won't say his last name) and we said no. She said he was from Edmonson and joined the Navy. He served his country and was then discharged because he got with another sailor of the same sex. When she finished the story, I remembered something my mom had said about a serviceman in bed with another serviceman and how she said they were no longer welcome in the church. I asked this girl what had happened to them and she said the last she'd heard was that they'd moved somewhere far away.

I've never told my therapist this but the clearest memory I have of that night is what Shaye said when the girl stopped talking. She said she was planning on going far away, too. It's strange how we don't listen to the signs when they're there, but they become so clear to us afterwards.

After that night, Shaye refused to admit we were together to anyone. Sometimes she would even tell me that she wasn't my girlfriend. I knew she was in pain, but it didn't make it any easier. Eventually this pain started to weigh down on me. I couldn't hold her hand when I wanted to, I could only ever kiss her in private, and I had to tell my parents that she was just my best friend. Every day I loved her more and more but I couldn't tell anyone about it. I've already told you it was worse when I convinced her telling my parents would be a good idea, but the anger Shaye felt after that summer carried on into our senior year. It bubbled until it exploded and we got into huge argument behind the bleachers at school. That's when Ben Clark saw us. It was because I had told Shaye that she shouldn't be afraid to kiss me, and that if she loved me, she would. Out here in the open where it didn't matter if anyone saw us. This was one of the biggest mistakes I have ever made in my life. Shaye did kiss me. It was probably the best kiss we had ever shared. Looking back, I think it was because it was our last kiss before everything changed. After that day, we were never the same.

I never wanted to go to school again. Not just because of the taunting or the names or the things they would say, but because I saw what it was doing to Shaye. The hardest part about her anniversary has always been the pain. And thinking about the reason all this pain exists. I pulled us both out of the closet when I should have just waited. I guess I didn't want to wait, because I had this idea in my head that we shouldn't *have* to wait. Now, the more years that pass, the more the pain doesn't even feel like mine. It's as though I am still carrying Shaye's pain for both of us because she isn't here anymore to bear it.

At the end of our session today, my therapist left me with a question: "How much of the pain you carry inside is yours to carry?"

I thought about this on the train back to Long Island. I am sad, but who isn't? My dad gets sad sometimes, my friends get sad, even my teachers get sad. The only difference is that they do not punish themselves for being sad, and I do. My heart is breaking at my own hand and I want to stop, I really do, I just don't know how. I wanted to ask Alex what he thought about this, so instead of going back home, I went to campus. Since I have started talking to Alex, I find myself in the campus library more often, even on the days that I don't have class. If I have work, I will go back to campus after my shift. I just want to know if there is a letter waiting. If there's not, I will leave another one for him. Just in case he's having a bad day, too. It probably sounds stupid to you, all these letters. I should just get his number and text him. But I like writing things down. I feel better for it. I also thought about telling my therapist about Alex today, but I didn't. Part of me felt like it was Shaye's day, and the other part felt like I still want Alex to be our secret. When I stopped by campus on the way home, there was a letter waiting. He had written back to the question I left on Tuesday.

Punishing yourself for being sad can bring you undone. I think you are your own worst enemy, Kayden. I want to help you be a friend to yourself

I didn't even think people like him existed anymore.

Thanks for listening,
Kayden

53

October 15, 2012

Dear Keeper,

I am not sure if you remember, but two weeks ago I wrote to you about Sleepy Ears. Well, the show was awesome. I begged my friend Tyler to go with me because Nate was on a spontaneous date with Bridget and if he gave up the date to come to the gig with me, she would probably kill me. Tyler got high before the gig even started (at like 6pm), but I didn't care because I was thinking about Alex. I asked my dad to wash my white shirt yesterday but he washed it with colors. So consequently, I wore a pink-stained shirt. I knew that I wasn't going to be able to pick Alex out of the crowd because I don't know what he looks like, but I was still hoping. Tyler and I danced all through the show and afterwards he bought me a hotdog from a stand outside the venue. I didn't end up eating it because he was super hungry and ate both of ours, but I didn't mind. Tyler has wavy hair that he sometimes puts up in a bun but mostly he just lets it hang in his face. He also likes wearing Joe's skinny jeans. Tonight he had pushed all his hair in a beanie and his curls looked more like little blonde clouds on the side of his face. He also wore a red and white striped shirt and a few times I asked him, "Where's Waldo?" and he laughed so hard I thought he was going to fall over.

I feel great. I wasn't sure if it was the music that made me feel good tonight or that Alex was probably watching too. My therapist once told me that sometimes we connect with people through sadness. She said we can feel those people with us even when we are not physically together. I think she has always meant it as a way for me to still feel connected to Shaye, but tonight I felt connected to Alex. Like we were just two people who had both struggled for a long time.

The library doesn't close until 9pm, so after the show I made Tyler wait outside while I dropped another letter to my textbook.

I wrote,

My dad stained my only white shirt so that it's pink. I'm sorry. Next time I will wear bright yellow!

Now I am listening to Tyler snore on my bedroom floor. For the first time in years, I don't feel like listening to my radio. I think I'm going to buy the Sleepy Ears album for Alex so I can leave it for him with my next letter.

Thanks for listening,
Kayden

October 19, 2012

Dear Keeper,

Marianne is Kip's daughter. She died from cancer ten years ago. Around that time, Kip created a conservation group called "Project Marianne" because his daughter loved marine life too. The project organizes lots of community events like beach clean ups, courses on water and habitat conservation, and stewardships to protect the plants and marine animals that live in the marina and the beaches surrounding East Point. The family was (and Kip still is) well known in town. When he is not working at the Center, he spends a lot of time talking to other students in the area about conservation. On my twenty-first birthday, we had a glass of whiskey together. He told me he used to drink bottles of it after Marianne died, but now he only has one glass each year. He said my birthday called for a celebration, but I can still remember the burn as I swallowed the stuff. Then Nate came to pick me up because they were all taking me out for dinner. Before we left, Kip gave me a bracelet that says "To live" on it. He said that it had belonged to Marianne and he wanted me to have it. He told me to keep studying things that are living so that I won't spend so much time thinking about dying. He looked sad and I didn't want to tell him that I wasn't thinking about dying, so I put the bracelet on and I have never taken it off.

Today at work, some kid tried to put a starfish in his pocket. Kip was handling the rock pool area and told me over the walkie talkie. Starfish aren't fish, they're actually echinoderms which are related to sea urchins and sand dollars. Sometimes I explain this to patrons, and I will use the term sea star. I like to think they are the stars of the sea, but honestly if they had teeth, I'd be worried. If you ask anyone at the Marine Center what their favorite part about working here is they will all say interacting with the animals. We have to methodically feed the sharks and rays every day and log all their food. I enjoy doing this with the other keepers, but what I like even more is getting in the water.

After feeding time today, I sat in Ray Bay and answered

people's questions. I want to say I do this because I like telling people about the display, but I'd be lying. The real reason I sit in here is so that I can watch the rays, especially Mahala. When I walk from one end of the tank to the other, Mahala moves with me. We are earth and ocean, separated but connected. Kip says I should not get emotionally attached to the animals, and I know he's right. But with Mahala, things are different. She sees me. She knows my secrets just by looking at me. With Mahala, the glass tank between us doesn't exist. I can share anything with her, even if she never talks back. It has been a long time since I have felt drawn to another living being in the way I feel drawn to Mahala, a magnetic pull that draws us closer and closer even if we are separated by language and water.

After Shaye died, I spent a lot of time wondering where she went. I knew where my mother thought she went but I didn't want to consider that. I thought maybe she was somewhere people aren't as cruel and you could be whoever you wanted to be. My dad says that sometimes life doesn't work out for everyone. That some people were never meant for this world, they were just passing by. I still think about if that's what Shaye was doing. When I look at the rays and see them passing through the tank, it weirdly reminds me of her life. Just passing by.

A small boy came up to me about twenty minutes into my sitting in Ray Bay. He had braces and lots of freckles and what I think was a German accent. He asked me if sting rays could fly. I told him no. Then he said he thinks they can because they have wings. I told him they are a different type of wing. He seemed to consider this before telling me I should put trees in the tank so they feel "more at home". If Mahala had eyebrows and had heard the conversation, I am sure they would be raised. When you spend enough time with the animals, you begin to understand and recognize their personality traits. Mahala is calm most of the time, but she is curious. I wish my thoughts were as calm as Mahala. Also, do you think you can feel drawn to someone you have never met? I don't know why, but Alex makes me feel safe.

After work, I stopped at campus to return another textbook I had borrowed. When I checked the desk, Alex had left me a letter and a photo. The letter mostly talked about the gig and his week, but at the end it said,

Don't wear yellow, here's what I look like. Me & Morgan

I was so excited to see what he looked like. He was smiling so big in the photo. I don't recognize him from around campus and I don't think he is in any of my classes. He had never mentioned Morgan either, but she was the girl in the photo. She's very pretty. The kind of pretty that makes your heart double over. Of course, I am not going to tell Alex this, because he might find it weird. Especially if Morgan is his girlfriend. In the letter, he asked to meet up on campus after classes on Monday. This means I am going to be nervous all weekend. At least I am working tomorrow and Sunday because Kip says the seahorses should be giving birth sometime this weekend and I am excited. I've never seen seahorses give birth before.

Thanks for listening,
Kayden

October 22, 2012

Dear Keeper,

I can't stop crying. I keep telling myself to stop but I just can't. Today was a disaster. Alex was horrible. He pretended that he didn't even know me. We were meant to meet just outside the library after my eco class. I waited for thirty-five minutes and he still didn't show up. I walked all over campus looking for him. I even went to the track, where I barely ever go except to watch Nate's lacrosse training or home games. When I had given up and was walking back to my truck, I saw him with a group of friends. The first thing I thought was that maybe he had his days mixed up. Usually I would never go up to people I don't know unless I am forced to, but the adrenaline had kicked in and I went over to him.

I asked him if he'd forgotten that he was supposed to meet me. I don't think this was the best opening line, but I've never been good at introducing myself, usually one of my friends does it for me.

Firstly, he said, "Do I know you?"

And then I said, "It's me, Kayden!"

The next part really hurt because he replied with, "Who?" and his friends laughed uncomfortably.

Then one of them said, "Do you know this girl? Selina will kick your ass, man."

I didn't know who Selina was or who any of these people were. But that wasn't even the worst part. The worst part was that Alex wouldn't even look me in the eye. My thoughts were screaming at me and my heart was pounding so hard, I thought I might have a panic attack. So I just ran as fast as I could. I cried so hard on the way home, I could barely see out of my windshield. My radio has been blaring but it's not making me feel any better. The songs are sad songs, then happy songs, then sad songs, then happy songs, all over the place like my thoughts.

Three weeks after I moved to East Point, my dad had to tow an old truck from Jersey to his shop. He had asked me to go with him. It's only about a three-hour drive, but it rained on and off and made me feel like the seasons changed three times. My dad was wearing a baseball cap and ripped jeans and he looked twenty years younger. It made me think about what kind of person he was before he had me, because I've heard parents say that you change when you have children. I'll always remember that trip because he called me soft. He didn't mean soft like a marshmallow, he meant soft like I don't like to yell a lot and I feel things, maybe more than most people do. I wanted to ask him who gave me this softness and if they could take it back, but I just stared out the window. After a while he asked me what I was thinking about and I told him Mom.

I remember he asked me if I missed her and I said yes but I missed the mom I had before I came out.

Then he said, "Your mother does love you."

"No, she doesn't."

"She does, Kayden, don't say things like that."

"She hates that I like girls, she has always hated it."

He kept his eyes dead on the road, "She just doesn't understand it."

"You do."

"It took me time to process after the initial shock."

He'd never told me this before, and I became angry at him.

"It's not like I had told you I'd killed someone. Why did everyone have to make such a big deal about it?"

"Well because I had to realize that I wasn't going to be some big burly dad fighting off some boy you brought home. I had to realize it was going to be different."

My anger softened and I said, "Well, I could have brought a burly-looking woman home."

He had laughed and reached over to clip my chin.

Then he got serious and quiet, "It was in your eyes."

"What was?"

"The sadness. The disbelief when Shaye was gone, I saw it. I saw how much you loved her, so I thought that despite everything your mother was saying, she was wrong. You loved Shaye just as much as you could have loved any man."

"I wish Mom could have seen it like that, too."

He said, "She sees the world different, that's all."

"Why are you on her side, if you left her?"

"I'm not on her side, Kayden, I just don't want you to think your own mother doesn't love you."

"My own mother doesn't even know me."

Which is still true. Four years on, our calls are irregular and I only see her once a year. When she does call, the conversations are short and they are difficult. Like she doesn't know who she has called and I don't know who is on the other end of the phone.

The last thing my dad said on that trip was, "Do you even know yourself yet?"

We drove the rest of the way home in silence.

I am thinking about that trip now because I don't want to be soft anymore. If I am not soft and I can't feel, maybe it wouldn't hurt as much as it does right now. I thought I knew Alex and it turns out I had been wrong. Things just don't make any sense. I have kept every single letter. I keep reading them trying to find the part where he could be cruel or playing a joke on me, but there is nothing. There is nothing in his letters to suggest that he was just pretending to be my friend or wasn't interested in what I had to share. I thought he understood sadness in the way that I do. I didn't think he would use this to only embarrass me in front of people. I wanted so badly for Alex to understand, to share my secrets and not run from me. Yet when we came face-to-face, he made me feel the way I have felt every day since Shaye killed herself: alone.

Thanks for listening,
Kayden

October 23, 2012

Dear Keeper,

Last night when I wrote to you, the thoughts were so loud I didn't think anything was going to calm me down. Things have drastically changed and I need to explain why.

This morning I realized the textbook I used to hide Alex and my letters to each other was still in the library. I am always losing things. I've lost my car keys, my wallet, my textbooks, my mind. After class, I went back to the library to get my textbook, and there was a girl sitting at the desk. I found this strange because usually no one sits there.

I said "Excuse me," because I didn't want to disturb her, and then I said, "I just forgot my textbook."

When she looked up at me, I had that feeling you get when you recognize someone but you are not sure how or from where.

"It's about time you showed up!"

As far as I knew, I hadn't planned to meet any of my classmates after the lecture, so I replied, "Have we met?"

"You're kidding, right?"

I was very serious, mostly because I was still upset from yesterday and I had already called in sick at work so that I could go home and sleep until my stomach stopped churning. But something about her felt familiar. After a few minutes of looking at her and the color of her eyes and the way her hair fell around her face, I realized it was Morgan, the girl in Alex's picture.

"Morgan!"

Her mouth sort of fell open and she frowned, which was a good indication that something wasn't right. She also looked confused. I was *very* confused.

"What?"

I said again, "You're Morgan." And then I also added, "The girl in Alex's picture."

She said she wasn't Morgan and then she laughed and asked if I really thought she was Morgan. I was getting frustrated because I had already told her. If this person wasn't Morgan, then I was clearly embarrassing myself *again*.

"Your friend or boyfriend Alex left me a photo of himself and you. We've been talking through letters."

Then I got mad because she burst out laughing and said something like, "It would have been easier just to get your number and text you. Here I was thinking we were being poetic."

"We were being poetic…" and at that point I trailed off because everything made sense.

"Alex?"

When she grinned, and nodded yes, I nearly fainted. Then she said, "Kayden, how could you possibly think I was Morgan?"

"You're Alex?" I said again.

"Yes!"

Then Alex stood up from the desk and moved to hug me. She gave me this tight squeeze and told me that I was the most poetically confused person she had ever met.

When she hugged me, I knew it was Alex. She smelled of strawberry and lilies and I am still thinking about her scent. I am also still thinking about how much of a psycho I must have looked to this Morgan person.

Alex is a *girl*. When she wrote "Me & Morgan," I had assumed she was on the left, but Alex was actually on the right.

I remember asking her to tell Morgan how sorry I was, but this only made her laugh again and hold me tighter.

Even though this was by far the stupidest error in judgment I have ever made, it felt good to be held the way Alex held me. It was like someone had been searching for me and was relieved to have finally found me.

Thanks for listening,
Kayden

October 26, 2012

Dear Keeper,

To tell you the truth, I was not expecting Alex to be, well, Alex. She graduated college a year ago with a degree in business but still hasn't decided what she wants to do. I guess life can be like that sometimes: it's a certain way all this time and then it's not. She works at Green Leaf, a cafe in town. Once I went there with Nate before we started to go to Shakedown's regularly, but I am sure I would remember if Alex had been working there. Alex's mom works in the career office at college and her *brother* Morgan is in his second year of a bio technology degree. Her hair falls down her back, and the ends are pink. She wears dark blue eyeliner if it's raining and has a tattoo on her wrist. When she was a teenager, her father died in a car accident, and ever since, she has been really close with her mom and Morgan. When she told me about her father's death, I wanted to tell her about

Shaye, but I didn't. When Alex talks to me, she doesn't talk to me like I am this sad chapter of a tragedy. I am scared that if I share all my secrets, this will change.

Today was the second time I have been to Green Leaf in three days. The first was the afternoon we met properly and Alex said we should get coffee. The second was the next day when she asked me to get breakfast with her before she had work. Then the third, this morning when Alex texted me (because this time we did exchange numbers) and told me to meet her after her shift. Of course, she didn't tell me Morgan would be there as well until he walked in grinning from ear to ear. Alex had obviously told him all about the psycho girl on campus. We sat in one of the booths. Everywhere smelled like cinnamon. Morgan was friendly and he apologized.

"I had missed out on an A for my chem report by one point. I was pissed and I'm sorry I took it out on you."

I think I shrugged, trying to act like it didn't matter, when thinking about how I had felt that night still made me shudder.

"It's fine, you probably thought I was crazy, talking about letters and that you knew me."

He laughed. Morgan has a deep laugh, the kind of laugh that comes from the belly, and the sound fills the entire room.

Then Alex interrupted him. "Don't laugh at our letters."

"Sorry, sorry."

"Although that moment in the library was… interesting."

Alex looked at me as though there were fire in her eyes.

I thought I needed to defend my honest mistake.

"But I really thought you were Morgan. It was the way

you wrote 'Me & Morgan' on your photo."

"Should I have said, 'My brother Morgan and I'?"

Alex leaned in towards me from across the table and I lost concentration before I managed to say something like, "Yes, grammatically speaking."

She was full of confidence, which was something I was not so full of, and it set off something inside me and I couldn't look away.

"Do you charge for your grammar services, Kayden?"

I remember blushing very hard and I was glad Morgan called the waiter over.

Have you ever had a double cheeseburger? I mean of course you probably have, but have you ever had a double cheeseburger from Long Island? I am telling you, they are something else.

After the food, Morgan excused himself to talk with a friend he spotted on the other side of Green Leaf, leaving Alex and I alone.

"Do you feel disappointed?" she asked.

"No, I quite like the food here."

She smiled, and said, "Not the food, I'm talking about me."

"What do you mean?"

"That I am really Alex?"

"No," I replied. In fact, I was feeling rather relieved, but I thought that would be a weird thing to say considering this was only the third time we had met in person.

"We should hang out tomorrow," she said. "Just us."

"Where do you want to go?"

"Anywhere."

There was something in the way she was looking at me that I couldn't quite tell if she was flirting or just being polite.

"I can take you to the marina," I said. "My friend owns it, lots of rock pools."

Her eyes lit up and she said, "You want to get wet already!"

I had been swirling a fry in ketchup and it flung off the plate when she said that. I was hoping Alex didn't notice, but to be honest, I think she was enjoying making me nervous.

I didn't answer her and instead I said, "I can teach you what I know about the ocean if you'd like. I can even take you into the Marine Center, I work there."

"Sounds perfect to me."

I'm hanging out with Alex tomorrow and it's just going to be us. I am excited but also have no idea what to wear.

Thanks for listening,
Kayden

October 31, 2012

Dear Keeper,

This is my fifth Halloween in East Point. Alex is arriving at my house in twenty minutes. I managed to fit into my freshman lab coat and I have covered it in fake blood. When my dad saw me I could see him panic, and then I reminded him it was Halloween. This sounds dramatic, but I suppose I would be like that too if I had lived with someone like me for all this time. When my parents were not divorced and we still lived in Edmonson, my mom would make a big deal about Halloween. It was her favorite time of year. We'd go to Costco's and pile candy and chocolate into the cart. Then we would come home and decorate the house together and carve pumpkins. My mom always dressed up as the main witch from *Hocus Pocus*, and I was always a ghost or a ghoul or something similar. She would buy an extra bag of candy just for me and sneak it into my pumpkin bag when I wasn't looking. My mom and I never fought back then. Sometimes I think that maybe if I weren't gay, I'd still have my mom. But then I have to stop thinking about it because it makes me too sad.

Halloween in 2004 is my first clear memory of feeling attracted to another woman. A woman came to our door with her son that evening. He was only very little and dressed up as a bumblebee. He said very shyly, "Trick or treat," which my mom loved because then she could make a fuss of him. I will always remember this Halloween, because it was also probably the last one I spent with my mom. All the other Halloweens I was never home. My mom began talking to the woman at the door because they were from the same church group. I remember thinking the woman was very pretty. Not pretty in the way that I liked her eyes or her hair or anything like that. I mean pretty in the way I thought about her lips for the rest of the night and what it might feel like to be older and kissing them, instead of eating all the candy I had collected. I was only fourteen so I suppose I didn't really think anything of it, but this feeling was only going to get more intense.

Tonight, I have invited Alex to a party at Nate's house. All my friends will be there. By "all" I mean just Nate, Tyler, and Joe. In my sophomore year, when things were bad, I stopped talking to a lot of the people I had made friends with in my freshman year. For a long time, it was just the four of us. Until Nate started dating Bridget and now sometimes she comes and hangs out with us, too. But she only talks to me when she has to.

Alex sent me a text message of what she is wearing. She is dressed up as Sailor Moon and the outfit looks *really* good on her. She said she has also bought us bottles of wine. I don't really drink, though. I used to a lot after Shaye died. When I started college, Nate was the first person who asked me if I drink to have fun or if I drink to get drunk. When I told him I drink to get numb, he said I probably shouldn't do that anymore. Since then I haven't had much to drink. Nate knows about Alex, but tonight is the first time she is going to meet my friends. This sounds silly because Alex and I are only new friends as well, but I am nervous. I want them to like each other. It probably sounds strange to care about someone so quickly, but I do care about Alex. I want to be around her, and I hope she wants to be around me, too.

Happy Halloween.

Thanks for listening,
Kayden

November 1, 2012

Dear Keeper,

It's very early in the morning, and I just got home from walking Alex back to her house. It was a very long walk but the weather isn't as cold as it normally is this time of year. I can hear the birds in the trees outside my window. I feel so good. I know it's probably because of the wine, but it's also because tonight I had fun. I am excited to tell my therapist about it but I think I will leave out the part about drinking alcohol. I will tell you about tonight because there is lots to tell and I want you to know before I forget all the little details.

Nate only lives two blocks over from my dad's house, so Alex and I walked there in our costumes. There were lots of younger kids going to each house to trick-or-treat, so I'm glad I left some candy by the door in case they knock on my house and my dad answers. He's not that into Halloween, so I hope he doesn't play a trick instead. As Alex and I were walking, the leaves that had fallen from the trees were crunching and it felt like they echoed down the street. Everybody always says their favorite part about fall is the leaves crunching under their feet, and it's mine, too.

When we got to Nate's house, his older brother opened the door dressed as Darth Vader, which I guessed he would be because he always dresses as a character from Star Wars.

"Hey, John."

"Kayden! Are you ready to cross to the dark side?"

He opened the door and we stepped inside, and I also introduced him to Alex before he told us that everyone was in the back.

There were some adults at the party, but they were all mostly in the kitchen with margarita glasses. Nate's mom was also in the kitchen talking to someone with frizzy hair about her boob job. Alex thought this was super funny. Nate doesn't have any younger brothers or sisters but every time the doorbell rang, I could hear John yell out to try and scare the kids on the doorstep. John isn't athletic like Nate is. He works with their father in the family accounting firm. This makes it hard for Nate because when his dad gets drunk he says that John is the favorite son. Sometimes I think about what it would be like to have brothers and sisters and I wonder if this "favorite" rule exists or if it's just a feeling some siblings get when the other sibling gets more attention. I should ask Alex if she ever compares herself to Morgan.

Nate was dressed up as Bob the Builder. When he saw me he ran over and hugged me. I knew he had been drinking because he hugged me extra tightly, and usually he doesn't do that in front of Bridget because she gets jealous and then they fight.

"You're here!"

I said, "Your costume is hilarious," because it was, and his shorts were shorter than Alex's skirt.

Nate hugged Alex and said he was happy she was here too. Normally Nate always invites the lacrosse team and some other people from his classes to his parties. Some people end up getting high and others end up making out, and one time, a girl who I can't remember the name of puked in Nate's swimming pool. His dad wasn't happy about that.

Around 11pm, Joe and Tyler were in the kitchen eating

chips. Alex was sitting on the counter and I was explaining the difference between manta rays and stingrays to her. Most of the time my friends do listen to me, even when I ramble sometimes. But Alex *really* listens to me; she didn't take her eyes off me the entire time I was talking. I thought maybe I had something on my face, but afterwards she asked lots of questions. Then this guy whose nickname is Mit came into the kitchen. He's a midfielder on the lacrosse team and I have only ever spoken to him once at a house party last year. He started talking to Alex.

"Where you from?"

Alex said, "Here."

"East Point, really? How come I've never seen you at our games?"

"Probably because I graduated a year ago and I don't really care about lacrosse."

Then Mit laughed as though Alex had been making a joke, even though I think she was just telling him how it is. People are very strange when they are drunk.

"I am the best player on the team."

Actually, in my opinion, Nate is, because he's the one that attracts the scouts, but I didn't say this out loud.

Alex said, "Really?"

"Yep, I put it down to how big the boys are."

He lifted up his arms and flexed obnoxiously. Mit has big arms, which is a good thing because it means he is better at his sport, but he shows them to lots of girls according to Nate. Which some girls like but others don't. I was hoping Alex didn't like them. I don't know why I felt jealous, but I did. I was wondering for the next few minutes if Alex would always like muscly arms or if maybe one day she could like my arms.

"I'm going to the bathroom," Alex announced and then she jumped down from the counter. Mit was too drunk to realize that Alex had left the room, so he just stood there talking to himself. Then Joe and Tyler wanted a cigarette.

"Kayden, come with us."

So I followed them out and down Nate's front driveway to the road. It was a little chilly out but not too bad. I don't smoke cigarettes anymore, but I used to when Shaye and I would get drunk together. Now they just make my throat scratchy.

Joe was talking about how he wants a new truck and Tyler was trying to convince him to get a Ford, even though he prefers Dodge. My dad says Chevys are the best trucks because the parts aren't as expensive, but I knew Joe just wanted to impress us.

Then Alex found us and she was a little tipsy, but she wanted to talk to me about something. We walked away from Joe and Tyler back to the side of the house and found the edge of the porch to sit on.

She explained how she had heard Nate and Bridget arguing when she went to the bathroom and that it reminded her of her ex-boyfriend. When she told me this, I felt disappointed because I wanted her to be like me. Obviously, I couldn't tell Alex this, so I am glad I can share this secret with you.

Then Alex told me that her last relationship was unhealthy and it made her question a lot of things.

"What kind of things?" I asked.

"I just felt insecure all the time. He made me scared to be myself. He cheated on me and would then lie to me about it or sometimes he'd ignore me for days."

I said something like, "I would never ignore you," because I was drunk and it just sort of came out.

"I know."

"Do you think it's weird we met on paper?"

"No. People meet online all the time, it's almost the same thing."

I thought about telling her about Shaye again, but I didn't. So instead I changed the subject.

"What do you want to do?"

"Now?"

"No, I mean with your life. What do you want to do and where do you want to go?"

Alex said, "Everywhere," and then laughed. "I want to do lots of things that aren't here in East Point."

She started talking about her life after college and how working at Green Leaf was just about making money. And I listened because Alex had all these plans and all these adventures she wanted to go on. I am used to making plans, plans have kept me alive, but hearing her talk about adventures made me want to sit on the porch in this moment with her forever.

Then I felt her hand brush the side of mine. Alex didn't look at me at first, and I thought maybe she hadn't noticed. But then I felt her thumb graze across the top of my knuckles and suddenly my whole hand felt like it was on fire. She kept talking about how she wanted her own business one day and the dreams she had for it. I kept my eyes trained on her hand, because if I looked at her face I was afraid I was going to lean in and kiss her. A few minutes later I felt her hand slip underneath mine and it curled with my fingers. She was still talking but something in her voice had changed. She had been like a storm talking about its passion for the wind until, with her hand in mine, she was calm. I was so lost in the feeling of her skin and wanting to kiss her, I didn't even know what to do next. For the first time in a long time, my sadness was not the reason I was aching. After this happened, Alex wanted to dance inside, and so I followed her and we danced with everyone for a little, but I am not very good at dancing so I went back outside. It was well past midnight and lots of adults had gone home. I think Nate's dad was passed out and his mom was talking to some boys from the lacrosse team, which is a bit weird, but I don't comment about those things to anyone, and so I was alone in the driveway.

The sky was very pretty and the night was clear. Being away from the city means that there is less light pollution in East Point and you can see more stars. Standing in Nate's driveway, alone and looking at the stars, I didn't feel as lonely as I have felt before. I feel very small when I'm sad, and sometimes things are blurry and my thoughts are rapid. They fill my mind with questions that I can't answer and pictures that I don't want to see. But I didn't feel like that on Nate's driveway tonight. Instead, I wondered how many other people are sad when I am sad or confused when I am confused. I wondered what these people were doing now and if they were having a Halloween party. I wondered if they had too much to drink and if they were seeing blurry things and remembering things they didn't want to remember or if they were feeling warm things and laughing. I wondered how many of them had met a girl and wanted to know everything about her. Once Kip told me that we only meet a fraction of people here on Earth and the rest we will never even know existed. I wondered how many people I would meet and if they thought the same things I did.

Eventually Alex found me and said we should walk home. We didn't talk about how we held hands or anything. We didn't even talk about how our hands somehow kept finding each other as we walked. Eventually when I got to Alex's house we said goodnight and then laughed as we stumbled over our feet. She asked me if I was going to be okay to walk home and I told her I would be and that I liked to walk. It was a good party.

I have a therapy session in the morning and I also have homework. The ocean covers more than seventy percent of the earth but scientists have only uncovered about five percent of this. There is so much we don't know. That's how I feel about Alex. There are all these things about her that I don't know yet. Have you ever felt like that? Like you just want to know everything about another person? You lose sleep over it.

Thanks for listening,
Kayden

November 9, 2012

Dear Keeper,

The last time I wrote to you, the sun was rising and I was a little giddy from too much wine. When I saw my therapist that morning, I finally told her about Alex. She was interested in this and asked me how Alex made me feel. I said I didn't know yet, but I would think about it and let her know. Since then, I have spoken to Alex every day. I am not sure if there is a word for this feeling. When you receive texts in the mornings and phone calls on your breaks at work and a message to ask you how your day is. When you are thinking about someone through your day and knowing someone is thinking of you through theirs, too.

It was game night tonight and I asked Alex to come. She drove and we met Joe and Tyler in the bleachers. We were a little late but Joe said there had been more fouls than action. They were sitting in our usual spot near the concession cart.

"One day I am going to ask Ellen Roberts out."

I laughed at Tyler, "She already has a boyfriend."

"I know, that's why I said one day."

"I think Bridget would rather die than let one of Nate's friends date her best friend."

There was a small space between Alex and I on the bleachers, and she closed it. I could feel her thigh against mine, and if it wasn't for the screaming and the yelling of the crowd around us, I was sure someone would have heard my heart beating.

Then Alex asked why Bridget never sat with us.

Tyler said, "Because she hates us."

"She doesn't hate us that much."

"You're right," Tyler replied. "She hates you mostly."

I looked at Alex and shrugged. "She doesn't like that Nate's best friend is a girl."

"That's ridiculous."

Tyler agreed, "Exactly! Kayden is practically a guy."

I shoved him.

"Watch the fries!"

Joe was distracted, yelling things out at Nate and the rest of the team. Even though he has never played lacrosse in his life, he's always so into the games. Joe and Nate have been friends since high school. Sometimes I forget that there is someone who has known Nate longer than I have. The first time I met Joe was at a party. Nate was talking to a girl and I found Joe by the punch. He was looking at Nate like he was angry that Nate was talking to the girl. His eyes were red, and at first I thought he was high, but then I realized he had been crying.

I asked him why he was crying and he told me it was because he wanted someone he could never have.

And now I know how Joe feels. Every time he looks at Nate, he knows that Nate would never want him back. Every time he looks at Bridget, he knows that she has something he wants. All this wanting and never receiving. I will never tell Nate that I think Joe is in love with him. It's the kind of secret that isn't mine to share. Nate is lightning-fast on the field. But Joe's eyes always seem to be trained on him, following him up and down the field even with all the other players weaving in and out. It makes me think that if you want something, you would follow it anywhere.

After the game, we went to Shakedown's like normal, and Nate met us later because he had a fight with Bridget, which is also normal. I ordered the double cheeseburger and a milkshake, and Alex ordered the same. Shakedown's mostly sells burgers, fries, milkshakes, coffee, soda, onion rings, and sometimes you can get a triple sundae. I've only ever had the triple sundae once. It was one of those days where sadness holds you so tightly you think it will become you and you will become it. It was raining, too, heavy and dark, like the sky was just as sad as I was. When it rains in East Point, the puddles sneak up on you and the streets are quiet because everyone is inside trying to stay dry. I had failed my first test. It seems trivial now, but back then when I was stuck, I felt like my life wasn't going to get better. I had lost Shaye, and yet I kept seeing fleeting images of her everywhere, like I was haunted by memories that didn't even feel like mine anymore. I wasn't talking with my mom so I had lost her too, and then the failure of that test just made me wonder if maybe Shaye had the right idea. As I later told my therapist, ice cream can save lives. She seemed to agree with me on this. I had found myself at Shakedown's and the waiter told me I looked sad, and I said I was. He said the triple sundae could fix that. And it did. Even for just that day, it was nice to pretend my sadness could be cured with a bowl of ice cream.

Nate finally joined us half an hour later. He looked frustrated when he slid into the booth.

"She drives me crazy sometimes."

Joe asked if Bridget had used the too-much-studying excuse again.

"She works hard, man, she's just busy."

Bridget goes to school in the city and only comes back to East Point to see Nate and go to his games.

"What, so she can't make an effort with her boyfriend's best friends?"

"Oh Jesus, Joe, what do you want from me?"

I knew Nate was tired because he always snaps when he is tired.

Joe said "Nothing," very quietly, and then said he was going to walk home.

"Joe, I didn't mean…"

Joe left some bills in the middle of the empty glasses and plates.

He nodded at Alex and said, "Sorry, Alex."

There was silence for a while and Nate looked even more frustrated. There are things that you can't see when you don't know every part of the story, and this was one of those things.

Tyler said he had work tomorrow and took the last handful of fries.

"You want a lift, Nate?"

"Yeah."

I told Nate that he played a good game and that I would see him later this weekend.

"Be good, Peanut."

When they left, Alex ordered more fries.

"Why does he call you Peanut?"

"I first met Nate in the cafeteria because he tripped over my backpack. Then all around campus he kept bumping into me, literally. He always joked that I was super small so he couldn't see me. Then he just started calling me Peanut."

"So who's Charlie Brown?"

I remembering thinking this was really funny for some reason and laughing.

"You can be Charlie Brown if you want to."

I think this made Alex happy because she didn't stop smiling. We stayed at Shakedown's until early in the morning, and it was late before she dropped me off. I spent ages with her in the car. We had the radio on and we were talking.

Alex asked me what I was thinking.

I was too shy to say that I was thinking about her, so I said, "Manta rays."

Then she laughed and said, "You really like fish, don't you?"

I went red. I knew I went red because my cheeks suddenly felt on fire and my hands went all clammy.

"I just like the ocean," I said. "It's calming."

"Calm is nice," she responded. "Sometimes I can be a tsunami though." She had been looking directly at me and it made me weak. "Do you think you could handle that?"

"Tsunamis are always caused by shockwaves, and I can't say I would be a very good earthquake."

She laughed, and I was mildly relieved, because my response had left my mouth before my brain had a chance to retract it.

Then she asked me about my parents. I've never spoken about my parents' divorce to anyone other than my therapist, and I let Nate know some things, but not much. Alex is just easy to talk to. I can talk to her like I talk to you.

I told her what my favorite color was, the first time I got drunk, and the time my dad called me soft. I told her about Kip and more about the Marine Center and what I wanted to do when I graduated and that making sick animals better again makes me happy. I also told her that sometimes I was sad and it didn't go away for a while, but that I was working on it.

Then Alex looked at me with a softness in her eyes that I'll never forget. We hugged. It was the type of hug that makes you never want to let go. I took in her smell. She wears perfume that smells like lilies and I soaked in the way her sweater felt under my chin as it rested on her shoulder. We hugged for a long time, until her arms were the only things I wanted to remember. And then she leaned into my ear. She didn't need to whisper because we were alone, but she did anyway.

"Stay soft, Kayden."

I will never forget tonight.

Thanks for listening,
Kayden

November 14, 2012

Dear Keeper,

Today three of our staff members called in sick, so Kip and I had to clean the ray tank ourselves. The scale of the tank means this took most of the day. It's getting closer to the holidays which means the Center is becoming busier. People come from miles to see the displays and attend information and conservation awareness seminars. We even have radio commercials now. Dad always teases me about the jingle, "Bring the whole family to East Point Marine Center and be amazed as the boundaries between you and the ocean are suspended." I laughed the first time I heard it, too; it sounds like one of those Morgan Freeman documentaries, only he is a much better narrator. We also get a lot of community funding, mostly because we have conservation projects dedicated to threatened species around the marina and wider parts of Long Island. The CEO of a huge company also donated millions of dollars to the Center about five years ago. This enabled more space to be used to rehabilitate marine life. All the animals here have a story to tell, as the majority have been rescued from injury. Some have even been here so long that they've grown accustomed to all the people who visit the Center throughout the year. I wonder about the animals that go back to the ocean, if they ever think about us from time to time or if they miss us, although Kip says not to think about things like that.

Our filtration system turns out massive amounts of water every day. The water is tested and monitored (sometimes I have to) around the clock so that the animals feel at home. Kip says that's why East Point Marine Center is an extension of the ocean itself. Sometimes we joke that animals come here for vacation. We have an engineer team that works below the Center in our control room. They are always replacing filters and cleaning the pipes, which are our main arteries. I like thinking about the Center like that. We are a heart, circulating and pumping life all around us and helping the animals to get theirs back. When I come here, I feel my own heart pumping life around my body. Being here brings me back to life.

Last year, the Center took on some graduates from my college. Dad sometimes asks why I won't just consider an engineering career or staying and working with the animals at the Marine Center.

"Just stay in East Point, kid," he says. "You don't have to go anywhere else!" It makes sense to my dad because he grew up on Long Island. He went to college here, left, and then came back again. It makes sense to Kip that I would stay here and work with him, it even makes sense to my colleagues, but it just doesn't fit with me. I have always wanted the Marine Center to be the missing puzzle piece, hell once I even *prayed* that it was the missing puzzle piece. But there was a time that I was convinced my sadness was connected to places. All I could think about in those early years at college was finding my way to California. It would be sunnier over there. I would leave all the tears and the depression and the anxiety in Long Island. But the thing is, I said the same thing when I was living in Edmonson. I am beginning to realize that perhaps the sadness is in my shadow and it will follow me wherever I go until the day I stop punishing myself for it. I still want to go to California because I think about all the animals that are injured and endangered by human beings and if there were more places like our Marine Center in East Point, how much more of a chance at life that would give them. Then I think of Mahala and how she saved me and I want to repay her somehow. This is the only way I can think of doing that.

I had all this adrenaline pumping through me as I squeezed into the dive gear and suited up with Kip. Sometimes I feel like he ages every week, from the creases and the wrinkles across his face to his graying curly hair and beard.

"You ready, Rayden?"

"You bet."

"You watch those stingers, you hear me?"

"Stingers better watch me."

He laughed and hooked up his mask and oxygen tank.

Stingrays are fairly docile and curious, and if their reaction isn't to flee to somewhere dark in the display, then they will sometimes brush their fins past the nearest object. The thing is, that object is going to be me if I'm not careful.

As soon as it was decided that Mahala was unfit for release, she was moved into her new home here in Center. This meant Ray Bay was expanded dramatically. We also added another Plexiglass tunnel. It's bigger and longer because the exhibit was widened and made deeper. Sometimes I think about the millions of gallons of saltwater coursing through Ray Bay every day and my head spins. Aside from Mahala, we also have reef rays and stingrays, schools of tuna and ginormous grouper, sandbar sharks, and twenty-three different species of fish. The tank is very blue and filled with algae and coral ecosystems. I've heard stories of the other divers saying the stingrays will often pick up rocks in their mouths and then drop them as they swim overhead. There were no rocks dropped on me today, but something did happen that Kip later said showed there was a bond between Mahala and I. Of all the moments I have spent with Mahala, I have never crossed into her space. There has always been glass between us. But this time, the glass didn't exist. I know how to communicate underwater. They teach you the commands and signs during the course before you complete your diving certificate. Kip asked if I was okay about six times. But being in Mahala's space was more than just cleaning a tank, or working, or putting on scuba gear and floating in a giant display of marine life. It was about how it made me feel.

Alive.

Mahala came extremely close, so close at one point I felt the tip of her wing graze my back. She would glide past me, never straying more than a couple of yards from where I was working. I moved, she moved. Two magnets, no longer separated. I could feel her power, her rhythm, her wings as she sliced through the water. I wanted to stay there. I had no loud thoughts in the water. There was just silence. It filled every space, and all the thoughts in my mind were suspended. I felt at peace and I began to remember what happiness felt like. The happiness that starts in your soul and spills down to the tips of your toes and rises to make your cheeks pink. Everywhere I looked there was life. Life skirted past me in schools of fish, it glided above me as the other rays became curious, too, it was in Mahala's eye as she looked at me. I am still on some cloud nine, but I can hear Dad pulling into the driveway and he's bringing home tacos.

Thanks for listening,
Kayden

November 21, 2012

Dear Keeper,

Sometimes I will stay awake all night and wait for the sun. I think about other people in the world and wonder if they are awake and sad too. If they are sad or happy or just there. I haven't spoken to Alex in a few days because school has been busy and so has work. I miss the sound of her voice. My therapy appointment was scheduled this morning instead of tomorrow because tomorrow is Thanksgiving. In our session, I talked, but mostly she talked. She said that when we are sad and we meet someone, they might become a crutch. I might miss Alex because Alex is a distraction. When we are sad we try to find meaning in small things. We try to be productive and we are sensitive to music and films. I told my therapist that I watched Marley & Me last night and cried, but that was only because it was a sad movie. She agreed with me, it *is* a really sad movie.

My therapist calls all this depression. She says that depression can and does happen to nearly everyone. Sometimes it is mild and other times it is crippling. Sometimes it comes in waves and other times it stays for a very long time, and for some, it never goes away. She says that my depression is very rigid and to imagine myself on a platform. The train keeps coming, but I am afraid and so I will not board it. It is very lonely on the platform and dark and loud. When someone gives depression a name, I know that it is meant to make me feel better. Because then I can tell my dad or Nate or my boss and it might help them to understand. But this name doesn't feel right to me. It feels like I am the person who is waiting for the sun to rise, and when it does, sometimes I am happy about it and other times I am sad that is has. And I want to be happy about it. You have to believe me; I always want to be happy about the sun rising. But maybe life is not about being happy every time the sun rises. Maybe it's just about being okay on the mornings that you are sad and knowing that the sun will always rise again tomorrow.

I try to remember what life was like when Shaye was alive. But it feels fuzzy now. I've almost forgotten who I was back then. My dad says it's not about then, it's about now. He says cars are never the same when they break and are fixed, and neither are people. The only photo I have kept of Shaye is in a box of old things that sits in my wardrobe. We didn't take many photos together, and all the others just sort of disappeared over time. I used to keep the picture under my pillow, thinking that maybe it was all a bad dream I would wake up from. Until one day it ended up in a box of old things and now I don't think I could get that photo out even if I tried. It is hard to imagine moments existing forever because they are caught on camera. When I would look at that photo I would wonder how Shaye could exist in that moment forever when all her other moments had stopped.

My therapist told me to look at pictures of my friends and family. She said this will remind me that there are people on Earth that depend on my existence. Like I am a moment to be caught on camera for as long as life will run its course. I look at pictures of Nate on my phone and think how he always seems to look as though he has just woken up. He has gray eyes and wears the same blue shirt a lot. I look at pictures of Joe and Tyler and notice how quickly they can grow beards. Tonight, I kept scrolling until I reached the recent pictures I had taken of Alex on Halloween and at Nate's game. The last picture I came across was my favorite picture of her. We had been having lunch on the marina and she had looked away laughing at something I had said, but I can't remember what, and I took the picture. The wind was in her hair, her mouth was open, laughing, and she looked so beautiful. It makes me wonder if someone's smile could make you forget all the reasons you were ever sad.

Alex just texted me.

Thinking about you

It's so late, but Alex is still here for me. I like that she's here. It will be Thanksgiving in the morning. I may not get the chance to write because usually it's a busy day and Kip comes over. But I just wanted to say I'm thankful for you and that you're helping me.

Thanks for listening,
Kayden

November 24, 2012

Dear Keeper,

Girls can be very confusing. I am not saying *all* girls, and I am not saying that they are confusing *all* the time, but people seem to think that because I'm a lesbian, I automatically understand every girl on the planet. Like my dad for example. He said last night, "You're a girl and Alex is a girl, how hard can it be?"

I wanted to tell him *extremely* hard, especially because I have not asked Alex those questions yet, but my dad wouldn't understand these things like you do. Alex and I are friends, but friends don't look at each other the way we do. Friends don't spend nights sitting in the car until 4am and hugging for a long time or sometimes staring at each other for ages without saying anything. And this is the most important one: friends don't hold hands in the way that Alex and I do. I mean we don't hold hands in public or anything like that, but sometimes when we are at Green Leaf or in the library or in her car or my truck, I will feel the heat of Alex's hand near mine, and it will touch mine in the same way our hands touched on Halloween.

Remember when I told you about the Halloween party and that I was sad because Alex had an ex-boyfriend and I wanted it to be an ex-girlfriend because at least then I would know that maybe one day I could make sense of us holding hands? Well, I found out Alex is bisexual. We went to Shakedown's today so that I could study for a test on Monday. It is the first Saturday I have had off in a very long time and Alex only worked three hours at Green Leaf, so she met me. To tell you the truth, I am not sure even how we got onto the subject of sexuality. I think I was talking about Nate and how sometimes I think it would be easier if he just dated Joe as they had lots in common and Joe was really good to him and has never taken him for granted. Obviously, they are just friends, but last year Joe bought Nate front row tickets to a New York Lizards game, which was the best present he ever got. Not even Bridget has done something that nice for Nate, ever. Then Alex asked me if Joe was bisexual, and I said yes and she said she was, too. I told her about how my mom doesn't believe in being gay or bisexual or anything other than what her Bible says, and Alex told me that her grandparents don't talk to her anymore since she came out.

She said, "They're my dad's parents."

"It is hard for them to understand?"

She nodded and said, "They used to say, 'You are too young to be mixed up.'"

Then I said, "Maybe you should explain it to them like you get strawberry milkshakes all the time but then you might decide that you like the chocolate one, so you will go with that for a while, might stick with it, or maybe you might want strawberry again. But it doesn't mean you like the other less because you like both."

Alex laughed for a long time.

"I'm sorry that you lost them."

"It's not your fault. I'm probably better off without people like that in my life. They blamed Morgan, my mom, and I for a lot more than we deserved."

When Alex was in the bathroom, I ordered a strawberry milkshake and a chocolate milkshake to show her I was on her side. We shared them together, and she said that she hadn't met anyone like me before.

I wanted to ask her more about her ex-boyfriend, but I wasn't sure if I should. We drank both milkshakes and then I finally asked.

"When did you break up with your ex?"

Alex said, "Not soon enough."

"So, never should have dated him in the first place?"

She laughed again. Alex laughs a lot around me, but I don't think I'm that funny.

"It was on the anniversary of my father's death. Mom, Morgan, and I hold something every year, just something little to remember him. I invited Brandon, my ex, and he said he couldn't come because he was working. But the next day I found out he had gone to the bar with some girl."

"That's terrible."

Alex shrugged, "I knew all these things about him before we started dating, but I went there anyway. Have you ever done that? Seen red flags but ignored them?"

I said, "Yes." I feel like my whole life has been a series of red flags that I've been ignoring, and my dad, Nate, and my therapist were all hollering at me to start paying attention.

"What about you?"

I didn't want to lie to Alex, so I said, "She died."

Alex was very quiet for a moment.

"She died?"

"Yes. She killed herself."

There wasn't any other way to say it.

"That explains a lot."

Normally people say things like, "I'm sorry to hear," or, "How horrible," and then they treat me differently, like they need to be extra careful with what they say next. Even though I'm not the one that killed myself, Shaye was. When Alex said that, it surprised me.

"It does?"

"Yes. Something like that always stays with you." Shaye's death has always stayed with me. "Do you blame yourself?"

"Yes."

Alex leaned forward in the booth, her elbows touching mine. Her face was different, not in the way that she looked at me differently, but more in the way that she wanted to tell me something.

"I wasn't honest with you about my dad when we first met."

"No?"

"No. He didn't die in a car accident, Kayden, he..." her breathing increased and she looked at the table a lot, but when she finally caught her breath, she looked straight at me. "He and Shaye share something in common."

I said, "Oh." Because strangely this made a lot more sense about Alex, too.

"My mom never talks about it and neither does Morgan. I found him when it happened."

"Do you blame yourself?"

"Yes. I always wonder if there was anything I could have done, if I missed something that caused it."

I nodded. It was the first time I had met someone who understood the sadness I was carrying.

Then Alex said, "Thank you for telling me."

"I like sharing things with you. I have all these secrets."

"Me too. Keep mine safe, I'll keep yours safe?"

"Okay."

I trust Alex, because she is a lot like you. She listens, and not in the same way my therapist listens or my dad listens. Alex listens in the same way a secret keeper would listen, and I just wanted to say thank you again, because holding in secrets all this time has been very hard, and I am tired.

Thanks for listening,
Kayden

November 28, 2012

Dear Keeper,

There is much more to my job than most people think, but there is something about the Ray Bay exhibit that draws me in. When you have these beautiful animals swimming in front of you or overhead in the glass tunnels, you feel like you aren't on Earth. Like it's a completely different world. I want to spend my days learning about them so I can talk about conservation. They deserve to be here just as much as we do. I like to watch the people that pass through, too. The parents who try to explain to their kids all about the marine animals even though they are just reading the "fun facts" on the plaques around the room, the couples who are clearly on their first date, and the tourists who don't speak much English. Then there are the few who come here alone. I wonder why they are here and if they are looking for the same things I am. Tonight was amazing. I will tell you why, but first I need to tell you how I got there.

Debbie usually works front desk. When it's busy, most of the floor staff jump on her to ring up tickets so the visitors can go through to the Center. Usually when Debbie takes her lunch break and I don't have tasks assigned by Kip, I take over for an hour or so. Today was one of those slow days where I didn't mind ringing up tickets and trying to make small talk with the patrons, get them excited for their visit, things like that. Everything was going as usual until a man walked in with his wife. I knew he was from out of town before he even opened his mouth. Something in what he wore and how he walked. It's funny how you can tell a lot about someone from that. When he walked up to the counter, he didn't even say hello.

"Two adults."

"Certainly sir, would you like any…"

"Use these coupons."

He threw two slips of paper onto the counter, and one slid right off and out of my hands. I fumbled to catch it but ended up having to pick it up off the floor. He huffed at this, as if the whole thing had taken me a year and not fifteen seconds. I looked at the coupons and noticed they had expired over a year ago.

"Sir, these coupons are expired."

I was expecting him to be rude, but I wasn't expecting him to scream and shout and go red in the face. I suppose you never understand why people get so mad over the smallest things. Maybe he and his wife had just lost their house and they wanted to visit the Center for free because it was where they met. Or maybe someone they loved had died. Or maybe they were both dreaming of a life they would never get and wanted to escape. Or, as I came to realize at least five minutes into the man's persistent screaming, some people are just assholes.

"Sir, I am more than happy to give you a discount on two adult tickets you purchase today, but policy…"

"I don't give a shit about your policy, these are my coupons and I'll use them."

"I understand sir, but these needed to be used by August 2011."

He yelled at me for another ten minutes over the coupons. He called me lots of things, but it wasn't until he called me stupid that I seemed to tense up. I have been a lot of things; I still am a lot of things. Like anxious and sad and sometimes a little nervous. But Alex says these things don't make me weak and they don't make me stupid. I went very pale and this must have made the man angrier because he continued to repeatedly call me stupid. I was very relieved when Debbie walked in the door, even if she had spilled mustard all down her polo shirt from her lunch. She told the man to calm down, and when he didn't, she told him to leave. The man and the wife left, and I could still hear him yelling all the way out to the parking garage.

Debbie told me not to worry, and I managed to hold in my tears and run to the staff room. Kip came in and asked if I was okay. I said I was fine even though I wasn't, and he could tell. He told me to take the afternoon off.

Normally I drive to work, but my truck is getting repaired (again) at Dad's shop. I missed the bus, so I walked. It's a long walk, but I had my radio turned up and I was trying to stay calm. I texted Alex the whole way home. When I got out of the shower, she had called me a few times, and suddenly my doorbell rang. She was at the front door.

"Grab your coat, its cold out."

I didn't feel like going out because I was sad, but Alex convinced me to go get dinner from Papa's, an Italian restaurant in town. East Point has a strip of restaurants and bars that look like cheap wine cellars, but they're pretty nice. I don't eat out much because Dad says he is going to try cooking again but always ends up bringing food home. Papa's was full of people and the waitstaff bustled around the room, filling up wine glasses and clearing away entree bowls and dishes.

When we got to the door, the hostess said, "We are packed tonight, ladies, but take a seat at the bar and we'll get you a seat as soon as we can."

I said to Alex that it was unusually busy for a Wednesday night, and she reminded me it was football season again and the Giants were playing. The bar was dimly lit and we hitched ourselves on the stools and discarded our coats on the bar. It was warm and my cheeks felt flushed, but this could have also been because Alex looked hot. I know that's not a very descriptive word, but she had on this blue dress with boots and nice earrings and her hair fell around her face like it usually does. She smelled like lilies again, and with the bar lighting and how good her legs looked, one crossed over the other, made my cheeks feel very hot.

She ordered garlic bread and we sat and ate and drank beer while we waited for a table.

"You aren't stupid."

"I know, but I still feel like shit."

"What kind of an asshole yells about an expired coupon and calls you stupid for pointing it out?"

"The kind of asshole that gets me so riled up I miss my bus and have to walk home."

"You should have called me."

"And said what?"

"'Come pick me up.'"

"I didn't want to bother you."

Alex tapped the side of her glass. "You don't bother me, Kayden."

I think I had a piece of bread caught in my throat or maybe I just lost my breath for a second because I had to chug some of my beer and it made my head swim a little. Again, I am speculating that it was the heat of the room and the alcohol that did these things, but I also think that it may have been the way Alex looked at me.

Then Alex said, "Let's get out of here," and she left some bills on the bar and grabbed our coats.

I asked, "Where are we going?"

She grinned and then replied, "Mimosas," and she slipped her arm around my waist as we went tumbling into the street. "They make everything better."

We ended up at Square Canary's which is this small bar just off the main strip. I think Nate brought me here when I had recently turned twenty-one, but I don't remember much of it, least of all the dark, leather-lined booths and the patterned wall hangings. Although I do remember the karaoke and the fairy lights and that each of the bartenders seemed to sport the same kind of beard. Alex had slid across from me in one of the booths. She looked at the bar menu first and then closed it quickly.

"Fries and Mimosas," she had said, and I agreed.

As Alex sipped the mimosa, her lip gloss left a small print on the edge of the glass. It made me think of her lips, and I stared at them as she spoke. We talked about lots of things like her favorite music and what her dad did before he died.

I talked more about manta rays and she laughed when I told her they sometimes jump out of the ocean like giant flying pizzas but no one can figure out why. I talked about my mom for a little while, what she was like before she knew I was gay. I didn't realize I was touching my radio as I spoke about her, but Alex noticed.

"Do you always carry that radio?"

"Yes."

"Why?"

"It makes me feel better."

"The music?"

"No."

"Then what?"

"Because only one frequency works, so I can't change the songs," I replied. "I can never tell whether a sad song will play or a happy song."

She looked at me from across the table and I thought she was going to lean across and kiss me.

"I like knowing that some songs will be sad and some songs will be happy, but neither of them last forever. It means my sadness won't last forever."

"I like you, Kayden."

"I like you, too."

And Alex did kiss me. Hard. She smelled of mimosas and mint and her hair fell all over my face. I have dreamed about kissing Alex since the moment we met, but it wasn't a huge deal when it actually happened. It just happened. It was soft and I felt her hand as it touched the side of my face and her thumb as she traced my lips after we had stopped kissing.

She whispered, "Let's dance."

I can't remember much else because Alex is addicting, and when you are addicted to something, everything else seems to fall away.

Thanks for listening,
Kayden

December 1, 2012

Dear Keeper,

Our lips have more nerves than any other part of our body. I think this explains why we feel things when we kiss. Even if we kiss strangers, we still feel a burning inside, right down to our toes. Kissing Alex felt different. Kissing Alex felt like my entire nervous system was set on fire. Alex is currently in the shower and I am trying to think about something nice to do for her today. I want to do something to say thank you for the other night. We went to Nate's game yesterday, and they lost for the first time this season. They played New Jersey College, who they have played before many times, but for some reason I could tell Nate's game was off. He missed passes and goals that he would usually make easily. We met him in the parking lot after the game and Bridget was yelling at him. I am not sure what she was yelling about, because she stopped when Joe and Tyler walked up. Alex and I were a bit behind because she was still trying to finish her corndog and I was in the middle of laughing at the mustard on her face.

I don't know what Joe said to Bridget, but it made her angry and she started yelling at him. Then she started saying bad things, like commenting on how he looked and saying that he was too weak to be Nate's friend. She used another word, but I don't want to say it.

Then I said, "Don't call him that."

Bridget threw her hands up, "Of course Kayden is here, always at every single one of Nate's games like a fucking leech."

I looked at Nate but he didn't look at me, he was looking at the ground. I wanted him to say something or do something, but he acted like he was frozen in time.

Then I told Bridget that Joe, Tyler, and I would always be at Nate's games because we're his best friends. This only made her yell more. She yelled about how he never does what she wants and never comes to visit her and it's all about East Point and his friends in East Point. She also said we had a super boring town and everyone in the city thought it was this small-town piece of nothing. I told her if it was nothing then why do we have so many people coming to the Marine Center and then she said, "No one wants you here, Kayden, you should have just killed yourself years ago."

Alex threw the rest of her corndog at Bridget and called her a bitch. She said something else like, "Get out of here before I knock you out." But I wasn't listening because I was thinking about what she had said.

Then Joe called Nate an asshole who deserved Bridget, and when he pushed past us I knew he had started to cry.

Tyler went after Joe, and Bridget stormed off. I thought Nate would follow his friends but he didn't. He looked at me with this pained expression on his face and went after Bridget.

I said something like, "Why does he always choose her side?"

And Alex said, "Because she's the one having sex with him."

"She speaks at us like we're nothing."

"That's because she feels like she's nothing."

Then I said, "Why would she be jealous of me? I'm gay and almost always on the verge of a mental breakdown."

Alex laughed and told me she would drive me home. She turned her car radio off and told me to put on my radio. We listened to Pink Floyd and Stevie Wonder and Alex knew the songs. There was something about the way she sang and how she laughed when she mixed up the lyrics. When we pulled up into my driveway, I didn't want her to leave, so I told her to come in for some tea and something to eat. She ended up staying over. Nothing happened or anything like that. We haven't even kissed again, but we fell asleep in my bed. I don't remember the time, but I remember waking up with her arm around me. When Alex touches me, I feel like the ocean does when it washes over the sand. Like there's a current moving inside me that I have never felt before. I have felt stuck for a very long time, and now I can feel parts of me working again. They are rushing and overlapping and moving in a way that feels incredibly good. My leg had pins and needles so I shifted and tried not to wake her, but she woke up anyway.

She asked, "Are you okay?"

I said, "Yes."

"You feel tense."

"I'm always like that."

I felt her smile into my back. "Why?"

I said something like, "Because I have a lot of secrets."

"Are you going to tell me all your secrets?" she asked.

I think being in the dark made me feel less nervous because she couldn't see me.

"I've probably told you more than anyone else."

"What's your biggest secret?"

I had already told her about Shaye, but I said something that caught even me by surprise. Something I haven't told anyone, not even you.

"I'm afraid of my own sadness."

Alex was quiet for a while and I thought maybe I shouldn't have said anything.

"You want to know my biggest secret?" she asked and her voice sounded sleepy.

"Sure."

"I am, too."

I found her hand and I held it until we fell back asleep.

My dad always says that when he was in his twenties he would take one step forward and ten steps back. He said life felt like the good things were the hardest to achieve and the bad things would come around as predictably as your taxes. He said this doesn't change as you grow older but that your perspective can. Alex understands sadness in a way that I do not. I hope she can teach me a few things. But for today, I am going to introduce her to Mahala. I want her to feel what I feel, one step forward each time Mahala cuts through the water. Alex has walked back into my room in just a towel. I am going to sit here and stare at these pages pretending to be reading until I can get my breath back.

Thanks for listening,
Kayden

December 8, 2012

Dear Keeper,

Fall is slowly drifting away and winter is returning for another year. The wind is getting colder and we are expecting snow to start falling soon. My truck groans very loudly in the mornings and takes a long time to warm up. Dad still thinks I should trade it in for something else but it was my pop's (he was my dad's father, the one who gave me the radio) and he's not with us anymore, so I can't seem to part with it. Nate was sitting on my front porch when I came home from work this afternoon. He looked sad, but I was still angry at him and we hadn't spoken in a week.

"Why are you here?"

"To say I'm sorry."

"You've been saying that a lot lately."

After I was released from the hospital, Nate came over to my house a lot. We watched old movies, because, other than infomercials, there wasn't much on regular TV and my dad won't pay for cable. The old movies made me feel better. Soon it became something we did a lot. Some of our favorites are *A Street Car Named Desire*, *The Wizard of Oz*, and *The Day the Earth Stood Still*. Tonight, I put on *The Wind in the Willows*, mostly because Nate secretly likes the animal characters and I thought it might make him laugh. I made us sandwiches, too, and let him speak about the off-game he had last week and his term paper that he has due soon. I didn't talk about what happened after the game last week because I could tell he had been high at some point during the day and he only does that when he is sad. His eyes were all red and puffy, so maybe he had been crying, too. Halfway through the movie he fell asleep. I tried to be quiet and not laugh too loud, even though Eddie Bracken's voice is hilarious in this film. Eventually my dad came home and was mad about some job he was working on today and he was banging drawers and cupboards around in the kitchen which woke Nate up.

"What time is it?"

"Eight or so."

"Shit."

"You never fall asleep during The Wind in the Willows."

"We broke up."

"What?"

"Bridget and me, we broke up."

I was quiet and then I said, "Why?"

"Come on, Peanut, you know why."

I was still quiet.

Then he sighed and said, "Cause she's a bitch."

"Did she dump you?"

"Yeah."

"I'm sorry."

Nate laughed and said, "No you're not."

I did feel bad because I didn't want Nate to be upset, but I was also glad. "You're right, I'm not."

He laughed and thumped me with the couch cushion and I was half grinning, half trying not to.

"And I think Joe is in love with me."

I wasn't expecting him to say that and I didn't know how to react. It's like when someone spills coffee all over the carpet and you either jump up and make a fuss or you are quiet and try not to make them feel weird and uncomfortable.

Nate continued as though he was unleashing everything he had been holding in. "Bridget thinks so, too, that's why we were arguing. He's been my best friend since we were fifteen. I think I have always known, but I'm selfish. I want him to always be my best friend so I don't say anything."

"Do you love him, too?"

He laughed, "Not in the same way."

I knew Nate wasn't gay, but it always helps to check.

"You ever think about what it will be like after college? When you move away and when I go wherever I am going and Joe and Tyler go wherever they are going?"

"How do you know I will move away?"

"You can't stay here, Kayden. You were never going to stay in Long Island."

I was quiet for a while. "I think about graduating a lot, where I will go, if we will keep in touch."

He said, "Yeah," and stared at the blank TV screen for a while. "It's just all so small, you know." Then he grinned and said, "Like you."

"Shut up."

"Nothing seems like it matters when you know the real world is coming."

Then it was my turn to say, "Yeah," and stare at the blank TV screen.

"Are you still seeing your therapist?"

"Yes."

"Is it getting better?"

"Some days."

"And the others?"

I shrugged and said, "Not so much."

"Wish I could help, Peanut."

I said, "Sometimes I think I don't need helping," because that was the truth. "It's like sadness is just an old friend who wants to hang out from time to time."

Nate hugged a couch cushion. "Doesn't sound so bad when you put it like that."

"Then why am I so angry at it all the time?"

"We get angry at our friends when they make us feel things we don't want to feel."

I smiled and said I wasn't angry at him, just at Bridget.

"I know, but I still should have stood up for you."

"There's lots of things we should do. I should stop being sad, but sometimes it's just out of our control."

Nate didn't say anything for a long time, and we both watched the blank screen as though the movie were playing again.

"Kayden?"

"What?"

"Don't let sadness take you away, okay?"

"Okay."

I wish I could stop being sad, I really do.

Thanks for listening,
Kayden

December 19, 2012

Dear Keeper,

Kip says that people are like the sand and sea. Sometimes we are on the shore, and the ocean pulls away from us. But if she truly trusts us, she will always return. Today, I helped Kip move into a different house. He is downsizing because he had this great big home with his wife and daughter, but neither are alive anymore so he doesn't see a point in keeping all those empty rooms. It was chilly and cold today, so I didn't mind warming up as we heaved boxes from Kip's truck into his new house. The house smelled musky, like someone hadn't opened the windows in a long time. I opened all the windows and fixed some of the drapes and made sure the sun could wash in. Eventually we managed to pile all the boxes into the living room and drag the couch and some furniture in there as well. All the glass items and ornaments had been wrapped in newspaper, but not very well. I was half expecting bits and pieces to be broken. There were large boxes and small boxes and they were labeled with different parts of the house.

I was going through boxes labeled "Photo Albums" and I found a picture of his wife, Harriett. She was beautiful, wearing a bright yellow dress and smiling. It made me think of Kip's life with her. Had he known within a few moments of meeting her that she was going to be the woman he loved for the rest of his life? I thought I would be with Shaye forever, but if I had met her now, I don't think I would have loved her in the same way. I have asked my therapist if she believes in fate, and she deflected the question back to me.

"Do you believe in fate?" she asked one early morning, when I had missed a shooting on 5th Avenue because the train was late and I had to take a short cut. I am still undecided. Mostly because I don't know if maybe I would be happy all the time instead of sad if I had met Alex when I was seventeen. But maybe we weren't meant to meet until now, after everything, because she's meant to *show* me how to be happy again. Something I haven't told you yet is that Alex's ex-boyfriend has been texting her. She brought it up the other day when we were in her car. We do that a lot now. It's usually her picking me up in her old Volkswagen because my truck works about two out of nine times in a good week and also because I'm on the right side of the highway, so this way I don't have to double back to get Alex. Then we usually head out to the marina and park the car for a while. Sometimes we will get hot chocolate from a local shop and other times we will go to the sushi bar in town. A few nights ago, we got sushi for dinner and parked her car out by the marina. It was so cold and the heating in her car wasn't working properly. We had fogged up the windshield with our body heat and warm breathing.

I said something like, "The windows are so foggy and we aren't even making out," because I say things without thinking. But Alex told me to kiss her, so I did. Things started to get a little intense and I remember wanting to take her clothes off but then her phone started going off in her pocket. It didn't stop either, and then when she reached to see who was messaging her, she went quiet. Probably the last person on Earth I expected it to be was her ex, so when she told me he had been messaging her lately, I didn't know what to say. I didn't say anything. Nothing at all about it, I just went back to eating my sushi. Sometimes I wish that there was a button for courage, and in the moments you don't think you can say what you want to say, you just press this button and it makes you say it.

Thinking about the other night made me lose my concentration on unwrapping Kip's silverware. So I said to him, "Alex's ex-boyfriend has been texting her. Should I be worried?"

Kip thought a moment, then said, "Well, have you asked Alex to be your girlfriend yet?"

"No."

"Then why would you be worried? She isn't your girlfriend."

Kip is old. I mean he's not that old, but he's old enough to think people still ask things like "go steady with me". I feel like Alex is mine, but maybe people don't belong to each

112

other anymore. Even though I want the words to come out, every time we're together, they don't. I am still trying to figure out if it's because they aren't meant to or because I am afraid. I don't want to be afraid because I don't want to lose Alex.

I said, "I just don't want to lose her."

Kip looked up from the old photo album in his hands. "Rayden, you of all people know how short life is."

I mumbled something about how that was true, but just because life is short doesn't mean we should go about giving people the power to hurt us without careful consideration.

"Well, if I was always so careful, I never would have never even asked Harriett to marry me. Her father was a real difficult man!"

"But what if Alex is still in love with her ex?"

"Then she's still in love with her ex!"

I pointed out to him that he was meant to say something like, "Oh how could she be when she has been spending time with you?" but he told me he's never curve-balled anything around me, and he's not about to start now.

Kip has always said I would have liked his daughter. He says he probably wouldn't have been able to stop us from talking about marine life all day long. We spent the rest of the day moving things into cupboards and drawers and looking at old photographs. When you have someone else's life laid out in front of you, it makes you think about your own and where you are headed. I wonder if one day I will have a wife and children with moments stored in photo albums.

"Kip, did you ever want to go with them?"

He sat down in an armchair and sheets of newspaper fell from the arm rests.

"Once," he replied. "It was just after Harriett passed and I wondered if she had found Marianne yet. I remember thinking to myself, if they're all going to be up there without me, that just doesn't seem fair."

"What made you not think about it, all the other times?"

"Little bit of faith, lots of distraction, and knowing that it wasn't my time just yet."

I let out a long sigh and fell into the couch. "Why do I think my life is hard when you have it worse?"

He went off at me the way he usually does when I say something he doesn't agree with. "Don't you go saying things like that!" And then he launched into a big speech about how I shouldn't compare myself to others, least of all him, or it will undo everything I have been working towards.

I said, "I don't know why I do it."

"You just worry about your journey. Don't pay any attention to anyone else other than your own unless your paths cross, you hear me?"

I said yes and then I told him that he needed to do something about the god-awful wallpaper in the house which made it look like something straight out of Doc's living room in Back to the Future. He made me carry the heaviest box into the kitchen for saying that. I think I've strained every muscle in my body.

Around dinner time, I was hungry and Dad texted me about bringing home pizza. I said goodbye to Kip and he told me that the otter handler is transferring to an aquarium in Georgia and moving his whole family from Long Island over the Christmas break. This means our Marine Center would be hiring a new otter keeper sometime early next year. I said something like, hope they can handle the otters' sass, before I ran to my truck because the sleet had started falling, and if it gets caught in your hair and dribbles down your back, it feels like it soaks right through to your bones.

Thanks for listening,
Kayden

December 22, 2012

Dear Keeper,

People in our neighborhood have been decorating their houses with lights and Christmas decorations. There is just enough snow for sledding, and Christmas carols are being played on the radio and in nearly every store at the mall. I have left Christmas shopping right until the last minute because I have been working, but Nate said we would go to the mall tomorrow. Everyone is in a rush all the time and parking spaces are hard to find and the lines are ridiculously long, so I am not looking forward to it. I want to get Alex something, but I don't know what. If I get her something big it might freak her out, but if I get her something small I don't want her to think that I don't care about her as much as I do.

Earlier in the week Kip and I decorated some of the displays at the Center with tinsel and we managed to put a tree up in the ticket lounge. I was hoping to finish early and spend time watching Mahala, but one of the octopuses escaped again. We have three Giant Pacific red octopuses at the Center. The one that escaped is called Jupiter, because even though he is red like the others, he has a white spot just underneath his beak. You are probably wondering why I keep naming the animals. I know I shouldn't do it, but it's just a poor habit. I grow attached to things. The police found Jupiter after raiding a house just outside of East Point. Kip told me the homeowner was arrested, and he had all sorts of marine life cramped in one small tank, some of which can't be housed together for behavioral reasons. It was horrifying. Octopuses are incredibly intelligent. Jupiter has memorized the movements of the security guards at night time, and for a long time, we couldn't seem to work out why all the angelfish in the tank opposite the octopus exhibit were going missing. I will give you a good guess. We amped up tank security, but it appears Jupiter managed to break through the duct tape. He left a slippery mess on the floor leading to the coral reef display. The funniest part was that he was sitting in his tank as though nothing had even occurred. Kip and I laughed about it over lunch. Sometimes I will pack two sandwiches, one for me and one for Kip. He asked me how I could ever leave East Point Marine Center where all the animals keep us on our toes. Every day that I become closer and closer to graduating, I think about if I should just stay in East Point. I am afraid that moving away from everything I have known the last few years will be bad for me. Each time I bring this up with my therapist, she asks me why I think this. She asks me a lot about what I think, which can be annoying because I just want someone to tell me what to do. There has been a small part of me that has all these plans, much greater than East Point. But now those plans feel strange because of Alex. How can you be someone for so long, and when you meet someone else, you feel like being someone more? Someone greater than you were before?

There is always evidence in Marine Biology. You come to conclusions because there is specific evidence to point you to that conclusion. If you can't come to a conclusion, it means you need to retest evidence or gather more information. Things that cannot be explained frustrate me, and when there are questions I cannot answer, I wish a simple equation would give me the answer. Not knowing how Alex feels about me is driving me insane.

Alex came and visited the Center after lunch. I wasn't expecting her, so when Kip called me on the walkie talkie to say she was waiting, I got a little nervous. I did take her to see Mahala that time I told you about. She loved her. She kept looking at me as I explained things that day, and it was nice to have someone so interested in what I had to say. But today she seemed different. I can't explain how. Like she was rattled over something. We went and sat near the turtle display, the jellyfish aren't so far away from there either, and I could see their glow in the corner of my eye. They were like the light at the end of the tunnel, only I chose to stay in the tunnel.

I asked, "What's wrong?" after a while of silence.

But Alex said, "It's nothing."

So I believed her.

I got home and I wanted something to distract me, so I dragged out all the Christmas decorations and put them up around the house. Dad has said since the beginning of December that he would do it, but he is always so busy and tired. In Colorado, I used to tree shop with Mom and Dad, back when we were a family. I haven't had a real tree since I moved out to Long Island. Our tree now is smaller, and the white specks all over it aren't fake snow, but dust. It spends all year up in the attic and only comes down for a few weeks a year. I feel sorry for it, even if it's not real. I put all the ornaments on the tree. Most are broken so I left them in the box. My radio played the whole time and old Christmas songs took turns filling our living room. Do you like Christmas songs? My favorites are *Little Drummer Boy* and *Last Christmas*. I just like the way they sound. I usually always think about my mom and Shaye around Christmas time, but this afternoon all I could think about was Alex. Now it's almost midnight and I have been writing a paper for my oceanography class. I haven't been writing it very well, because I'm so distracted. Earlier tonight when I was decorating, I took a photo of the mistletoe I had hung from our mantelpiece and I sent Alex a photo of it. She responded to it just now, which I wasn't expecting because I thought she would be asleep. She said that she wants to kiss me. Then she said— wait I need to read this.

She said she wants me to spend Christmas day with her family. Wow. I wish you could see this on my phone to make sure I am not hallucinating. She added, "my whole family" at the end of the message, which I think is her way of emphasizing. I don't know if I should take a bottle of wine or some Doritos. Dad and I don't do anything fancy for Christmas, we mostly just get take out. But we get *lots* of take out, as well as dessert because it's a special occasion. I texted Alex back.

Okay, that will be nice

Dad and I always wear really tacky Christmas sweaters on Christmas morning, but I don't think I can wear the same thing to her family dinner, because mine says, "Merry Christmas, ya filthy animal."

Thanks for listening,
Kayden

December 25, 2012

Dear Keeper,

This morning my dad tried to make egg nog. It tasted a little like the way milk does the day before its expiration date. We opened our presents, and it turned out we both got each other coats. He laughed about it for the rest of the morning, telling me I was becoming more and more like him every year. I drove to Kip's house to give him the present I had bought him, and he hugged me. You can tell a lot about someone from the way they hug you. Kip only ever hugs me on Christmas. It's the kind of hug that a father would give his daughter. Then Dad drove me to Alex's house. Last Christmas he bought me this funny looking reindeer backpack, which I was glad I had today, because it could fit my notebook and also Alex's present inside. I wanted to surprise her later tonight.

"You gonna be okay, kid?"

I said, "Yes," and told him not to worry.

When I knocked on the door, Alex answered. She was wearing jeans and a blouse that dipped low at the front and made me lose all the words I was going to say. She was also holding egg nog.

She said, "Merry Christmas!" excitedly and rushed forward to hug me.

I asked if she had been drinking egg nog already, but she laughed and pulled me inside. Alex's house was very warm. There are lots of pictures hanging on the walls. The furniture is mostly solid oak and there are some big paintings on the walls with splashed paint. I asked Alex who they were by, and she said that her mom likes to paint in her spare time. Alex's family reminds me of my family, at least when things weren't so broken and everyone got along. Amy hugged me as soon as I followed Alex into the kitchen. I haven't been hugged by a mother in so long. It felt strange but nice at the same time.

She said, "Merry Christmas, Kayden," and I said Merry Christmas to her, too. Then Morgan appeared and he was also holding egg nog. He must have seen my face scrunch up because he asked whether I liked it or not, and I told him normally I did, but this morning I'd had the worst egg nog I'd ever tasted and I didn't think I would want any for the rest of the day.

Amy said they were going to her mother's house for Christmas lunch (Alex's grandma). She only lives a street away, which is a good thing because I was loaded up with roasted potatoes to carry to the house. I didn't mind so much because whatever seasoning Amy had used smelled so good.

On the way out, I noticed their stockings hanging from the mantelpiece. The last one had a name I didn't recognize embroidered along the top.

It didn't take very long to get to her grandmother's house. Amy said that it would have taken even less time if Morgan didn't drag his feet so much.

She turned to me as Alex rang the doorbell, "He always drags his feet. Make sure you lift your feet up high when you walk, Kayden!"

I replied, "Yes, ma'am," before the door was whisked open and a woman stood there wearing lots of bright jewelry. She had silvery hair pulled into a bun and lots of wrinkles, and I assumed this was Alex's grandma.

She also announced, "Merry Christmas, one and all!"

Alex laughed and hugged her tight, then Morgan, then Amy. I awkwardly hung back on the porch, unsure whether I should hug Alex's grandma too.

I said, "I'm Kayden."

"Honey, I know all about you!"

She kissed both my cheeks and squeezed me tight. I

didn't know what she meant about knowing all about me, but I couldn't ask because I was swept into the house as Alex began quickly introducing me to the people inside. I was still holding the roasted potatoes while all this was happening. There was her Uncle Peter and his wife Alison who have two kids. There was Jessica who is fifteen and mostly wanted to talk to her friends on her new iPhone. Then there was Luke who is younger, maybe eight, and likes Spiderman. He wanted to talk to me about this, and I tried to keep up but he spoke very fast. Then there was Amy's youngest brother, Dustin, who likes music. He liked talking about lots of songs that everyone else didn't know, but I did. I was finally able to put the potatoes down and then I was asked about college and everyone was very interested to know that I worked at the Marine Center. Especially Luke, who wanted to ask all sorts of questions, and so I told him about Mahala. The house smelled of herbs and pork and wine. There was also this smell coming from the kitchen which was minty and sweet and I couldn't work out what it was.

Morgan told me, "That's Grandma's secret sauce recipe. Once you try it, you will pour it over everything."

After another round of marine questions, I felt like I was talking too much, which is strange for me because I don't usually talk at all. So I decided to switch to nodding a lot and saying thank you when someone topped off my glass or handed me crackers and dip. Then it was 2pm and time for a late lunch. There were two long tables joined together in the living room near the tree and the fireplace. Mashed potatoes and gravy, roasted vegetables, beef, ham, chicken, and roast turkey were spread across the table. Alex's family makes a much better roast turkey than my dad. He tried to cook one for Thanksgiving last month, but it burned so bad we ended up ordering Chinese. This one was crispy on the outside and the stuffing was just right. I don't think Alex's Uncle Peter likes me that much. When he passed the potatoes, he said, "You aren't really like the last guy Alex brought over for Christmas."

And I said, "Well no, because I'm not a guy."

I was just pointing out the obvious, but Alex and Morgan laughed at the same time which made Uncle Peter turn red. Although he did seem much nicer and happier after a few glasses of Chardonnay. We had gingerbread cookies and apple pie and Christmas pudding for dessert. When I lived in Colorado, my mom would cook for Christmas and her parents would come over and eat with us. Mom doesn't have any siblings and I don't talk to her parents now. Dad's brother moved to China for work so he could never come with his wife and kids. Every family has a different tradition. The last real Christmas I had was when I was sixteen. Mom's parents came over and asked me what colleges I had applied for. I told them I didn't know, and they looked at my mom like she wasn't doing her job properly. All I remember was feeling like I wanted Christmas to be over.

But for the first time in so long, I finished all the pudding on my plate and even stayed at the table to finish my conversation. Even though that conversation was with an eight-year-old on Spiderman's different powers. In the late afternoon, we sat around the Christmas tree and Alex's family gave out presents. I even got a present from them, which I felt a little bad about because I hadn't bought anyone else presents, just Alex. But Amy told me that I didn't need to worry, as there was only one of me and whole lot of them. Still, it was nice of them to invite me for Christmas, so afterward I helped clean the dishes. I like Alex's grandma. She is very direct but also very funny. Alex found me in the kitchen and told me she wanted to show me something and we went upstairs. I hadn't given Alex her Christmas present yet, so I took my backpack with me. Her grandma has kept all her children's rooms the same. Peter's room had cowboys everywhere and also all his family's suitcases because they don't live in Long Island anymore. Dustin's room was full of action figurines from the eighties, and Amy's room was purple with butterflies hanging from the ceiling. She also had lots of books: Jane Austen, Roald Dahl, Amy Tan, Stephen King.

I said, "Your mom has a lot of books."

"She's read every single one on her bookshelf and on the bookshelf downstairs, and there's about fifteen boxes in the attic, too."

"Wow."

Alex smiled and sat on the bed. She was still eating some pudding from a bowl she brought upstairs. "Do you want some more?"

"That's okay, I think if I have any more pudding I will probably have my food baby prematurely."

She laughed. When Alex laughs, it makes me feel warm. Her shoulders rise up and down and the sound of her laugh reminds me of a Ben Howard song, soft and gentle like I could listen to it all night.

Then I noticed a picture of Amy in a wedding gown sitting on the bookshelf. I assumed the man standing next to her in a tuxedo was Alex's dad. I asked her what his name was.

She said, "Scott."

I realized that the stocking I had seen hanging in her house earlier had been her father's.

"Scott and Amy."

She nodded and finished her pudding. Then she said, "I miss him so much around the holidays."

I sat down on the bed next to her. "What was he like?"

Alex looked at me as though no one had ever asked her that question before.

"He was funny," she replied. "My mom has never laughed the way she used to laugh with my dad."

"When did they meet?"

"They were college sweethearts. Met in Mom's sophomore year, dated, married, and had us. I remember one night when I was six, Morgan suddenly spiked this huge fever. He was only two. Mom was at work because she used to teach an English night course, so it was just Dad, me, and Morgan. He was burning up so badly and was sweating so much it was like he'd been swimming. Dad piled us into the car and rushed to the hospital. He called Mom on the way, but Morgan started screaming in his car seat. Then I started getting upset. So Dad started making these siren noises and saying we are going on an adventure."

She stopped for a moment and I watched as she looked at the picture of him and Amy on the shelf.

"Anyway, we got to the hospital and everyone was fussing over Morgan and one of the nurses was super sweet to me and gave me candy. They managed to get Morgan's fever under control, and then Mom arrived. She was super upset until Dad disappeared and came back with these tomatoes. And he goes, 'Sorry honey, our kid went so red he transformed.'"

Alex started laughing and I laughed too, because it was pretty funny.

"And Mom got so mad at him, but then she started laughing. That was always the thing about Dad, he always tried to make the people around him, especially my mom, laugh. Since he's been gone, we don't laugh that much. Not until you anyway."

"Me?"

"Yes, you. You're so weird, it's funny."

If being weird made her laugh, then I would try to become even weirder if that were possible.

"After Dad took his life, there wasn't much reason to laugh. It got worse when I came out, because for a while my mom didn't understand and his parents thought it was because of her parenting skills. Like who I am is a direct result of my mom."

"My mom still says that. She says that it was her fault somehow, that she went wrong somewhere."

"My dad's parents, too. Things broke when Dad died because they blamed my mom. But they got even worse when I told them I liked women. Especially because I told them I could still love men as well. People tell me I have to just like women or just like men and that I can't like both."

"That's because most people are just scared, Alex."

"My dad wasn't scared. He would have never made me feel the way they have."

"Well I think he'd be really proud of you."

"You think?"

"Yes."

I stood up from the bed and opened my backpack. "I have your present, I said. Alex had given me a snow globe with a manta ray inside. I was so scared it was going to break in my bag, I asked her grandma to wrap it in a dish towel.

She grinned at me and said, "Were you too shy to give it to me before?"

I handed her the (badly wrapped) present and nodded, "Your family wouldn't have understood it."

When Alex opened my gift, she sighed. But it was the kind of sigh girls do when you do something nice for them. At least I was hoping it was for a full minute until she said it was the cutest thing anyone had done for her. When I went to the mall with Nate, I got Alex a Charlie Brown sweater. I wanted to get her this because in a world full of Mondays, she's the reason I look forward to them.

Then Alex asked me to stay over. She said, "Don't go home tonight."

"Are we staying at your grandma's?

She laughed and said, "No," but said sometimes they come back for breakfast because there's always so much food left over.

"Did you like the food?"

"Yes, especially your grandma's secret sauce."

This made Alex happy for some reason.

"I'm glad you came."

"Me too."

She leaned towards me and her nose was a little cold but her cheeks were warm and her breath smelled like pudding and egg nog.

"Guess what I have."

I said, "What?" quietly because my bottom lip had begun to quiver and I was trying to control it again.

Alex held out her palm with a leaf of mistletoe inside. I thought it was a piece of mint leaf at first, but when she kissed me, I felt like there would never be a better Christmas.

I texted my dad to see how he was because he was alone, but he told me he was at Kip's house drinking whiskey. It made me feel less guilty knowing they weren't alone on Christmas. So I told Alex I would stay with her. Before we left, her grandmother said she hoped she would see me again. I thanked her for having me, because that's always polite to do, and I left with Alex. It was cold out and it had snowed in the afternoon, which meant our footprints left a trail from Alex's grandma's house back to hers. We tripped coming up the driveway and fell onto her lawn covered in snow. We found this really funny, and Alex tried to make a snow angel. Then Amy and Morgan caught up and Amy told us to get inside quickly or we'd catch a cold. I felt the way I did when I was five and my mom was always there to look after me. We shook off the snow and hung our coats, and after a while our cheeks became flushed with the heat of Alex's house. We weren't tired, so we played cards downstairs with her mom and Morgan. Her mom was a little drunk which was hilarious, and Morgan won every hand, which Alex had said he would because he's good at cards. Then we said goodnight and went upstairs to her bedroom. I hadn't been in Alex's bedroom before. Usually we go to my house or to the marina or Green Leaf or the library. She turned the heat on in her room because it was much colder than the rest of the house and she closed the door. I was only wearing a sweater and my jeans. I had left my shoes downstairs and forgotten to wear my thick socks today, so I was cold.

Alex must have noticed because she said, "You're shivering, do you want me to turn the heat up more?"

I don't remember what I said, I just remember kissing her. I remember her hands holding my face and then moving to my neck and down my shoulders to pull me closer. I remember my heart beating so loudly, I was afraid Alex was going to hear it. I remember our breathing becoming heavier and how easily her clothes slipped off her body. I remember my hands shaking as I brought them down the length of her back and across her hips as I pulled them into me.

She whispered, "I want you," into my ear as she breathed into it and, "Take your clothes off," as she kissed my neck.

And I remember skin to skin, hands in places we hadn't dared to touch before, and my lips drifting over her thighs and in between her legs. I remember telling her that I wanted her too and feeling like I could do anything in that moment and wanting to stay inside her until she had lost all control.

Alex is asleep now. She has Ellie Goulding posters on her wall and a picture of her dad on her bedside table. She is sleeping in her pajamas but the material is so thin that if I fold into her I can feel the heat of her skin. I want to always be invited to Christmas lunch. Remember when I asked you how you could be someone and then meet someone else and want to be better than before? I think I know the answer, because every time Alex looks at me, I know I deserve to be happy again. It's just shy of midnight, so I'm not too late, and I wanted to say Merry Christmas. Hope you got everything you ever wanted, because you deserve that, too.

Thanks for listening,
Kayden

December 31, 2012

Dear Keeper,

It's the last day of the year and I've been thinking about how much sharing it will take for there to be more good days than there are bad. I've been trying really hard not to have bad days, but today Alex said that sometimes people just feel bad for absolutely no reason at all. I don't think people who struggle to exist want to die. I just think they don't know how to share.

I drove to Green Leaf today and I waited in my truck until Alex had finished work. Before I left my house, I scribbled thank you on a piece of paper and folded it. When she came outside, I called out to her and she looked up at the sound of her name. She smiled when I found my way across the road to her. Snow was falling and it caught in her hair the way my breath catches in my throat every time I see her.

"What are you doing here?"

I handed her the note.

"What's this?"

"A letter," I said, although it seemed obvious.

When she opened, it she looked up at me.

"Why are you thanking me?"

"Because lately you've made most of my bad days, good."

She folded the paper and put it in her pocket. Then she reached for my coat and pulled me towards her.

"Has anyone thanked you lately?"

"What for?"

She whispered, "Existing," before her lips were on mine and I could feel how cold the tip of her nose was but it didn't matter because everything about Alex reminds me that even if existing is hard sometimes, there are some things worth existing for.

I haven't been able to say this in a long time, but I'm okay. I hope you're okay too.

Happy New Year.

Thanks for listening,
Kayden

131

January 1, 2013

Dear Keeper,

Last night we went to Nate's house for a party. His parents have gone to California to celebrate the new year on vacation, which means Nate has the whole house to himself. I don't think he is sad about Bridget anymore because he has been talking to other girls. Joe, on the other hand, is a different story. Nate would never make Joe feel bad about his feelings. In fact, I don't think he has told Joe that he knows. But at the same time, this isn't going to stop Nate talking to girls, and when he is talking to girls I can tell that it hurts Joe.

It was snowing outside and the neighbors hadn't taken down their Christmas lights. The reflections looked like colors dancing in the sky. When Alex and I arrived, some people were on Nate's front porch smoking and they had a little smoke cloud around them. I hoped they would pick up the butts or else Nate's dad would come home and yell at Nate. We went around the side gate and there were already people in the hot tub and outside in the yard around a fire. I didn't recognize everyone, but they looked a lot older. I just assumed they were John's friends. Alex reached for my hand as we were walking and held it as we went inside. I should have asked her to be my girlfriend right then and there, but I didn't. Tyler was in the kitchen using the blender and talking with someone I didn't know. He smiled when he saw us and asked if we wanted a cocktail.

Alex asked, "What's in it?" and Joe said it was a special recipe.

"That means more vodka than juice," I said.

Then Tyler said, "Most people are in the living room or using the hot tub."

"But it's freezing."

"They're drunk."

Alex took the glass Tyler had poured for himself and sipped. She wrinkled her nose and looked at me before setting it on the counter and taking the blender from him.

"I'm taking over the cocktails."

"What's wrong with mine?"

"They're horrible."

I laughed and went to Nate's fridge to see if he had any more juice.

My dad once told me that how you spend your New Year's Eve was how you were going to spend the rest of the new year. I hope not, because after a couple of hours, things didn't go very well. Alex was sitting on the kitchen counter and we were talking with Tyler and some of John's friends. I liked this part of the night because I was leaning into her and every now and then she would kiss my cheek softly. If I could have spent the rest of the year and the next year and every year after just like this, I would. But then Joe walked into the kitchen and he was upset.

I asked, "What's wrong?"

"Nate just ran his mouth, that's what."

Tyler told him to relax and that made Joe even more upset.

"Fuck you, man, you don't know what this is like."

Tyler didn't know what Joe meant, but I did.

I said, "Joe, let's just go talk about it."

"I'm done talking, Kayden. He yelled at me and made me look like a dumbass in front of people."

I have never been good at knowing what to say. Usually I just listen and Joe will talk until he comes up with an answer on his own. But I don't think he wanted to come up with an answer. I think he was all out of them. I followed him through the house and I tried to make him stay, but he said that Nate was a jerk and he slammed the front door as he left. I told Alex that I had to go find Nate, and I went upstairs. I checked Nate's bedroom but he wasn't in here. The bed wasn't made and there were pizza boxes stacked on his desk. He is always so messy. Then I checked all the other rooms. I accidentally opened the door on a couple who were probably about to have sex and I said sorry awkwardly and shut the door as quickly as possible and tried to unsee the image I had just witnessed. Whenever Nate has parties in the house, he makes everyone promise they won't go in his parents' room or else he would start rumors on campus about them. Nate pretty much knows everyone, so if he said something, people would believe him. I figured that since I was his best friend, he wouldn't mind me checking his parents' room to see if he was in there. He wasn't in their room, but the bathroom door was open and the light was on. I peeked through the open door and found him sitting in the bathtub.

I said, "Hey."

Nate didn't say anything for a while, and then he said, "I didn't mean to yell at him. I'm drunk."

"I know."

"Is he still here?"

"No."

"Fucking hell."

"I think Tyler went after him."

"He can't just say shit like that to me in front of everyone."

"He's high."

"So what? You think when I get high, I go running my mouth like that?"

"No, but you used to leave people in parking lots and make them walk home and let your ex-girlfriend say horrible things to them."

"Peanut, that's not the same."

"Why isn't it? Do you think Joe wants to feel like this?"

Nate threw his hands up in the air. "You think it's my fault he's in love with me?"

"It isn't anyone's fault."

"Tell him that, and while you're at it, tell him to quit being so fucking angry at me."

"I'd be angry if I loved someone who couldn't love me back, too."

"When did this get so fucking messy?"

Nate curses a lot when he is drinking. It feels very strange to be writing with curse words.

"Joe has been in love with you for a while. He just didn't let his feelings show while you were with Bridget. But now that you don't have any commitments and you have more time, I think he just wants to spend time with you again."

"Kayden, I don't have time. We are graduating. You

135

think we have time to work this out? I want to make the reserve team before my dad forces me to become a part of his firm."

"I know, but Joe's been your best friend since high school."

"I didn't think it would turn out this way."

"No one thinks it's going to turn out any way, Nate. Things just happen."

He asked, "What about you?"

"What about me?"

"Well, are you going to apply for that marine program in California or not?"

"Maybe. I mean, yes, I am, it's just that moving to California sounds scary."

"Of course it's fucking scary, we've lived in a bubble for the last four years. Just us and the island."

I was also a little drunk so I started to think about how if the bridges collapsed and the tunnels caved in, I would be on Long Island forever. Then I wondered if I really could leave all my sadness in East Point when I graduated.

"I am going to apply," I said. "I want to get into the program and move to California."

"Then what's stopping you?"

"Alex."

"Alex is holding you back?"

"No. I mean I want Alex to come with me, but I don't know how to ask her to come to California with me when she isn't even my girlfriend."

Nate laughed then. He laughed for a long time and he

pulled his cup from the vanity and drank some more.

"Peanut, just fucking ask her out."

"Yes but—"

"No buts, just do it. You like her, she likes you, what are you so afraid of?"

I was going to answer, but then something sounded like it crashed downstairs and Nate swore loudly, but it was a word that I am not going to write down. He stumbled out of the bathroom and left me wondering why I was so afraid. I can tell you because maybe you will understand. In my heart, sadness has sat for a very long time. It has taken up a lot of space. I am afraid that there won't be enough room for Alex and that sadness will ask her to leave. I don't want Alex to leave, but I don't know how to tell sadness to leave instead. One of them has to go because my heart doesn't have enough room for both.

I thought Alex was going to be my New Year's Eve kiss, but at midnight I couldn't find her anywhere. I searched for her all over the house, and then when people started to filter out, I got worried. I texted her but she texted back telling me she had gone home. I have been trying all morning to call Alex to find out what happened and where she went, but she isn't answering any of my calls or texts. I don't know why everything is suddenly so messy.

Thanks for listening,
Kayden

January 4, 2013

Dear Keeper,

I wish I could tell you that the new year has been great, but I can't. Alex didn't return any of my calls yesterday or the day before that, and then today we went to the marina but she barely said a word. When I dropped her off at home, we had the biggest fight. We sat in my truck for an hour screaming at each other before she ended up crying and slamming the door. I'm trying hard to figure out how any of this is my fault, but somehow her getting extremely drunk and kissing another girl on New Year's Eve doesn't seem like my fault, even though she tried to say it was. I was barely able to drive home because I was crying so much. At the beginning of the party, she didn't leave my side, and then after I went to talk to Nate, I didn't see her again. I don't understand any of this.

When I walked in the door, my dad was halfway through his Chow Mein that he had ordered for the night and he looked confused.

"Hey kid, weren't you seeing Alex tonight?"

"I don't want to talk about it."

I slammed my bedroom door the same way Alex slammed my truck door. Then I heard my dad knocking.

"Kayden? What's wrong?"

"I just want to sleep."

My dad doesn't listen to me when I'm sad. He opened the door and I felt my bed creak as he sat on the edge.

"What happened?"

"Alex kissed someone else."

"Why?"

"She said because I didn't take us seriously, which doesn't even make sense because I invited her to spend New Year's Eve with me. I was going to kiss her at midnight."

My dad thought for a moment and rubbed the back of his head. He usually does this when he is trying to come up with an answer that he's not so sure about himself.

"I wish I could tell you that I had all the answers to relationships, but I'm divorced." He gave me one of his cheesy grins which meant he was trying to be funny.

"I feel like I'm seventeen again and I don't know how to say what I want."

"I'm forty-eight and I will always feel seventeen when it comes to that stuff, Kayden. There's no right or wrong answer."

"Do you think she did it because she doesn't want to be exclusive?"

My dad crinkled his nose, and I knew this is probably stuff I should be talking to Joe about, but he was still upset with Nate and didn't want to talk to anyone.

"I think you should go talk to Alex when you have both calmed down."

"She said it was my fault that she kissed someone else."

"Well maybe to her it was your fault, and to you, it's her fault. Right?"

I wiped my face with my sleeve and nodded.

"But you won't find out by screaming at each other."

"I really like her, Dad. I haven't felt this way since—" I

paused and he looked at me and I knew he knew what I was going to say next, but I said it anyway, "—since Shaye."

"Then it's something worth working out."

I said, "Thanks, Dad," when he hugged me, even though I was still feeling sad. He asked me if I wanted to watch the sports channel with him downstairs but I said that I just wanted to stay up in my room.

I hope the new year gets better because at the moment it sucks without Alex. She was so upset and I don't know what I did to make her that upset. I hope that it will get better.

Thanks for listening,
Kayden

January 9, 2013

Dear Keeper,

It has taken me nearly five days to figure out what went so wrong. Alex heard the conversation I had with Nate. The one where I said I wanted to move to California. The thing is, she didn't hear the part about how I wanted her to come with me. I found this out from Tyler when I went to Shakedown's. He texted me asking if I could help cheer Joe up. The three of us were sitting there not talking and then he asked how Alex was.

I said, "I don't know, we aren't really talking."

"Well of course not, you upset her."

"What?"

"Yeah, when you told Nate you wanted to move to California."

Then Joe said, "You're moving to California?"

"No. I mean, maybe one day. I want to apply for the marine program in California".

Tyler whistled and then said, "Alex clearly didn't hear that part."

I slumped in the booth and wanted to cry again.

"She was pretty trashed," Tyler added.

"But I didn't say I wanted to move to California without her. I haven't even applied for the program yet."

Tyler shrugged, "Just go figure it out with her, then. What are you so afraid of?"

"Rejection," Joe said, looking at me.

"She kissed another girl, that sends a pretty clear statement." I said.

Joe shrugged, "I don't think she wanted to kiss that girl, Kayden. I think she was mad and drunk. We do stupid things when we're mad and drunk."

"It's not an excuse."

"It's not. But what's your excuse for not talking about California with her sooner?"

I didn't really have an answer for that. "I just want Alex," I said and I looked at him. "Do you think she wants me back?"

Joe looked really sad, "At least she *can* want you back."

I wasn't even eating my fries, just swirling them around in the ketchup.

I finally wanted to know more and asked Tyler who the

girl was. But Tyler said he didn't know her. He just assumed she was one of John's friends, because she was older. At midnight, she grabbed Alex and kissed her and then Alex yelled at her.

"I saw the whole thing. She was pretty upset."

"Why didn't you tell me?"

"The hell would I tell you some other girl kissed Alex?"

I sighed because I was frustrated. And then I said everything is just super messy and I don't know how to explain things to Alex.

Joe told me he agreed with Tyler and that I should go see her.

"She doesn't want to see me."

It was Joe's turn to sigh and slump back in the booth. Then he said, "Ever since I've known you, things go on inside your head and no one has been able to figure it out until Alex. Not Nate, not me, not Tyler. And then this one person comes into your life and you're too scared to do something about it."

I wanted to tell him that it was because once you let someone in there was no going back, but I guess he already knew that.

"At least you got a chance, Kayden. I don't have any chance, and my friendship is most likely ruined."

"Nate doesn't want to not be your friend."

"That's not what I'm saying," he said. "I am in love with my best friend and he'll never love me back."

"You have a chance to make it right." Tyler said, and then he said, "This is why I love food more than girls. Less drama. Just goes in your belly and out—"

"I get it." I interrupted and I shook my head at him, but maybe he had a point. I wasn't sure where to find the courage or the words. I have never been very good at talking about things. Then I thought about writing it down, just like the way we met. So while Tyler ate and Joe watched him, I took a napkin and wrote down what I was feeling.

After Shakedown's, I drove to Alex's house to talk to her. I told her that the marine program was something I wanted to apply for, but that didn't mean I wanted to leave her.

"I'm really sorry."

"Me too."

I thought things were going to be okay, but then she said maybe things were the way they were because we were in different places. I didn't understand, because all this time she had said that no one understood her in the way that I do. When I got home, my dad had left a note to tell me he'd gone to the bar with some of his friends. I went to my room and I shut the blinds and I laid down. The ceiling is dusty and there are some small, glow-in-the-dark stars left in the corner from the previous kids who used to live here. When we look at stars, we are looking at light that might not even be there anymore. The light is still visible to us even after the star dies. I wondered if this was the same about people. If you connected with someone and they left, if the connection still remained. When I think about all the reasons Alex and I are not together, I come back to the same thing: fear. Is she just as afraid as I am? How can someone love you if you have too many secrets? It's been three months since I met Alex and I count all the days I stop myself from telling her that I want to be with her.

Now I feel like I have lost her, and the thoughts have never been as loud.

Thanks for listening,
Kayden

January 13, 2013

Dear Keeper,

It's still winter break. The car windshields are frosted in the mornings, peppermint mochas are still available at Starbucks, and our snow blower keeps jamming. I'm going to ask Alex to be my girlfriend. I want to feel things again, even the bad, and I don't want to be afraid anymore. I will tell you how it goes when I get back. I hope the next time I write, Alex will be my girlfriend.

Thanks for listening,
Kayden

January 15, 2013

Dear Keeper,

Something very bad happened, but I am okay. There are fragments I don't remember, but at least I am still here and I can write to you and tell you about what happened. When

I left the house to see Alex, it was dark and cold. Rain was falling and I remember thinking I should go back inside and get another coat, but I didn't. Normally I exit the freeway and take Johnson Avenue, but there was emergency night construction which meant I had to take the longer route out by the new development estates. The roads aren't paved so well just yet and there's no lighting because most of the properties are still being built. I was trying to rehearse what I wanted to say to Alex and thinking about what she would say. My radio sat on the passenger seat and The Temptations were playing. I remember distinctively the song was *My Girl* because I love that song. This next part is where my memory went in and out, like being caught in a rip tide, pulled in, then out, in, then out and I was somewhere in the middle trying to make sense of it. Something jumped in front of my truck. It was bigger than a squirrel because I didn't run over it, I ran *into* it. Dad said it may have been a deer, but that's not important. Then I swerved so hard, I lost control of the wheel. I remember this part like flashes happening all at once. I slammed into trees and into the worksite fence. Then my memory goes blank for a while.

When I opened my eyes, I saw my front windshield cracked like a giant spider web. Then I saw the tree the front of my truck had plowed into. It was tall with a thick trunk. I was bent over the steering wheel; my seatbelt had sliced the side of my neck and was holding me in place. The front of my truck was bent inwards, locking my legs under the dashboard. There was blood in my eyes and I could smell burning rubber. I could also smell lilies. When they open, they give a creamy and sweet smell. It smelled like Alex and it made me think of the sun and the sky and being alive. I didn't want to die. Then my memory fades to nothing. Not many people take that street at that time of night, so by the time someone found me unconscious at the wheel, I wasn't in the best state. I can remember a light, bright as it shone through my truck window. Then someone was tapping on the glass, and they said, "Can you hear me?"

I could hear them but I couldn't speak. Then they said, "Hold on, we've called an ambulance."

This part is mostly blank too, but I remember feeling very, very cold. Then I blacked out again.

When I opened my eyes next, there were flashing lights, red, blue, red, blue, and sirens. I became acutely aware of the pain when I saw the lights. It hit me harder than my truck had hit the tree. My shoulder was hurting, my head was throbbing, my legs felt heavy, and my neck ached.

Then there was a flashlight coming through the window. A person was speaking into a radio. They were repeating codes that I don't remember. Then there was more darkness but I could still hear things. I could hear my radio. The Temptations weren't playing anymore, but I can't remember what song I could hear. Then someone was tapping on the window of the driver's side again.

"Can you tell me your name?"

I whimpered and said, "Kayden," and then more darkness.

I woke up again as they were cutting me out of the driver's seat. This was the part I wished I had stayed unconscious for so that the memory of it wasn't so clear. I had glimpses of faces hovering around me, people talking, saying, "possible fracture, concussion, trauma wound to the head." Then the seat belt was cut and I was lifted onto a stretcher. I was put in a space blanket and I have never thought those things would make a difference, but they do.

I asked if I was going to die.

The EMT was female, and she said I was not going to die and that I was going to be okay.

I told her I didn't want to kill myself. I probably shouldn't have said that, but I wanted her to know.

Then darkness.

I woke up entering the hospital. There were lights flying overhead, more people talking, giving orders. I remember rushes and flashes of pictures like someone had fast forwarded a movie and I was trying to figure out the storyline but I was missing pieces. Then someone asked if my parents had been contacted. I started crying and asking for my dad. Then they administered more drugs, and I stopped crying. I was taken into a room with a big x-ray machine. They told me to do things but I don't remember doing them. Then there are more holes in my memory until I woke up nine hours later in the early morning. My dad's silhouette was asleep in the chair and I felt soft hair splayed over my arm. I was thirsty and my head hurt, but I didn't want to move. I knew it was Alex draped over me because I could smell her perfume. It was the same scent of lilies I had smelled in my truck. And I wanted to cry, because it was like she had been there with me and she was telling me not to let go. The machine next to me beeped loudly and I shifted.

Alex woke up with a start and realized my eyes were open. She started crying. She cried so hard and moved so that she could hug me. She kept saying sorry in my ear and kissing my neck but I didn't understand because it wasn't her fault.

I said, "It's not your fault."

"What were you doing out so late in the rain?"

"I just wanted to see you."

She started crying again and I tried to wipe her tears away but the IV machine kept getting in the way.

"Baby, you should have called me."

She was pinching the bridge of her nose as though she were trying to stop the tears from falling. I tried hard to listen to what she was saying, but I don't remember anything. I just remember the way she had said "baby" and how she had said it about me and how that made me feel. And even though I was in pain and my throat was cracked and dry, my heart was racing so fast I was worried it would set off an alarm.

"Kayden?"

My dad had woken up. His hair was ruffled and his eyes looked swollen and sunken at the same time.

I croaked, "Dad," and Alex moved so he could hug me.

"I'll get the nurse."

I knew he said this because he was about to cry but he felt he couldn't because he's my dad. I've seen my dad cry before, big heavy sobs, and every time he does, I want to tell him that it makes him braver.

Alex said, "You scared me, Kayden," and reached for my hand. I remember feeling her fingers knot through mine and how warm they felt. Even when she continued to talk I still can only remember her other hand closing over the top of ours and feeling like she was holding me in place.

There was a voice and then a nurse followed my dad into the room. This was the first time I met Nurse Shayla.

She said, "You're up bright and early, Kayden. Welcome back!"

I tried to smile, but it hurt. She knew I was in pain and she began to check things, and I was finally able to have some water.

My dad said he was going to go and get a coffee and I nodded. He tried to say something to me but he was on the verge of crying again, and I just told him to get one for Alex, too.

Nurse Shayla then said, "Your girlfriend stayed all night!"

"Girlfriend?"

Alex said, "Yes, that's me!" but her voice sounded high and nervous.

Nurse Shayla said everything looked good and that she would be back in a few hours along with the doctor looking after me. When Alex and I were alone, she reached for my hand again.

"They would only let family stay overnight. I had to say something or else I would have had to leave, and I couldn't leave you."

"I was coming to ask you."

"What?"

"The other night, I was coming to ask you to be my girlfriend."

"Kayden…"

I said, "Wait," because I had rehearsed this speech and I

couldn't remember it all, but I wanted to get the bits I could remember out in the open.

"I know that it takes me a while to say what I am thinking, and I know that I should have told you how I felt earlier, but I was just..." I lost the words because my head was aching.

But Alex said, "Scared," and I nodded.

She said, "Me too. I begged my ex for attention and I begged him to chase me and he never would, so I just wanted—"

"Me to do it."

She laughed and it made some of the pain disappear. Alex's laugh will always be better than any drug in the world. There were all these other things I wanted to say, but Alex kissed me, and, using all the strength I had left, I kissed her back.

Later Alex went home to shower and Dad had to go to the auto shop. The doctor came to see me in the early afternoon. Nurse Shayla came with him and she was checking things as he spoke to me. He told me my collarbone was badly bruised and I had seven stitches from where the glass tore open my forehead. If the dashboard had crushed even an inch more, my legs would have been crushed with them. There was a small cut on my neck from the seatbelt. The doctor told me I was very lucky. He told me that when I came into the emergency room I couldn't remember some things, like my dad's middle name and what street my college campus was on. He said that I would need to be assessed before they would discharge me. But I didn't forget the way Alex smelled or the shape of her eyes or the way her body feels against mine, so all the other stuff I wasn't very worried about. Then he asked me if I had driven the car into the tree on purpose. He had said it so flatly and without emotion. I told him, "No." He didn't ask me any more questions after that. Nurse Shayla told me I had to stay one more night. I didn't like that news very much. Before she left the room, she told me she goes on her dinner break at 8pm so she probably wouldn't check on me after that. She said she had told the same thing to Alex. I tried to stop myself from smiling but I couldn't help it.

There was another patient in the room as well, but she was very sick. I knew that it was something to do with her brain, because once around five in the afternoon her monitors started going crazy and I could hear her thrashing around in her bed. I called for the nurses and at least six of them came in to deal with the situation. I think she might have had a seizure but nobody told me anything. In a few more hours she seemed to be fine again. I think she didn't want to talk about it because she didn't want me to feel sorry for her. You can feel pity in hospitals. All these well people coming in to see the sick people and feeling sorry for them, or feeling sorry for themselves that the person they love is sick, or that their husband or wife is working late to help the sick people. Pity is almost as loud as the machines beeping.

I was finally discharged this morning. I am home, but Dad is fiddling around downstairs calculating how many days he can take off work, even though I told him he doesn't need to. He told me I'd had too much morphine and there was no more arguing. Alex has texted me all morning. She is at work but she is coming over tonight. I can't wait to see her. I just want to be next to her and beside her wherever she is. Kip came to the hospital because Dad tried to get away from the shop but he had a job this morning and couldn't. When he helped me into his truck, I asked if mine was okay. Kip sighed a heavy sigh and I knew I probably wasn't going to get my truck back on the road.

He said, "Don't think about that now, Rayden"

"How am I supposed to get to work?"

"Me."

"How am I suppose—"

"Listen here, kid."

And I'd hadn't heard Kip use that tone of voice since the very first time I started at the Marine Center.

"You're like a daughter to me, you know that? So don't you be worrying about things that can be taken care of."

"I didn't do it on purpose."

It was sunny outside and the light bounced off patches of snow and puddles on the pathways. The light poured in through Kip's window and it made the gray of his stubble look white.

"I know, Rayden." He looked at me with his dark brown eyes and said, "I believe you."

If you have ever been sad in the way that the sadness changes how everyone looks at you, if you have ever been sad in the way that it makes it impossible for people to believe you when you try to talk about the thoughts in your head, having someone believe in you is the single greatest feeling you could possibly have.

I was silent the whole way to my house. Then I saw my truck outside with half the bumper missing, the smashed window, and the dent on the right side, and I cried. I cried so hard that Kip had to hold me. I sobbed into his shirt and I made small tear circles and I told him that I wanted to live and he just told me again that he believed me.

Nate, Tyler, and Joe are coming over in another hour. I told Joe I didn't want him to feel awkward, but he told me that I was more important. I'm not sure if it's the painkillers, but I do feel important. I feel that I matter and that I don't want anything to happen to me because I don't want to leave Alex and I don't want to leave my friends or my dad. By the way, the Jello in the hospital was awful. But I would have awful Jello every day for the rest of forever if it meant I got a second chance at life.

Thanks for listening,
Kayden

spring

semester two

January 21, 2013

Dear Keeper,

The sadness has gone away. I don't know where it went, and I have been looking for it all week. Not because I want to feel sad, but because I want to know if it will ever come back. Last week, my therapist asked if I missed my sadness. I said I didn't, but I still wondered where it went. Where does sadness go when it is not needed or wanted? The days seem colder but it hasn't snowed all week. Spring semester classes don't officially start until tomorrow, but I missed out on enrolling in Oceanography 502 because the class was full, so this morning I visited Professor Martin to see if I could fit into her class. Nate drove me to campus on his way to practice. When I got to the lab, the halls were quiet. I found Professor Martin in her office, crying. I felt awkward so I knocked. She hurriedly wiped her tears and looked up as I walked into the room.

She said, "Kayden," with a huge sigh of relief. "I heard about your accident, how are you feeling?"

I figured my dad had called her. "I'm fine, better than last week."

"What can I help you with?"

"I'm taking Oceanography 502 this semester, but your class was full. I was wondering if there was a chance you could accommodate me?"

She looked at me over her glasses, "Still enjoying my lectures after all these years?"

I grinned and said I was.

She opened her desk drawer and took out some papers. Then she signed the printed line along the bottom of the page.

"Here's the paperwork, I've signed it for you. Just make sure to hand it in to student services no later than tomorrow."

"Thank you, Professor."

I was going to walk away, but I couldn't. I asked her why she was crying. I don't know why I felt like I had to ask her. She was quiet for a moment and I felt like I had crossed a line, but then she said her husband had been unfaithful and she had filed for divorce. The thing was, I could feel her sadness. It was separate from me because it was hers. For the first time in years there was this room full of sadness, but I was not a part of it, I was just there, watching. I said that I was sorry that this was happening to her, but she told me that it wasn't my worry to carry. She also told me not to get into any more accidents and we both laughed because there wasn't much else to do. Then she handed me another piece of paper. She told me she had written a referral for the marine program internship in California and to include her referral in my application. I thanked her again and I started to feel dizzy. Either because my head had started to ache again or because I was elated and excited, and they were feelings I was still trying to be friends with.

I thought about the divorce all the way home. I didn't want to wait around for Nate to finish lacrosse practice, so I took the bus and walked. I'm not sure why I thought about my professor's divorce so much. I thought about what kind of bad things had happened and why they had happened and that my professor was a nice lady and she had dedicated most of her life to her students and I wondered why her husband had been unfaithful. I don't know my professor that well, but I thought about why people hurt each other so much all the time. I thought about Nate and Bridget and Joe and Nate and my dad and my mom and I wondered if there was no such thing as selfishness, what life would be like. My therapist told me once to imagine my heart as a fort. It was my castle and my home. It was the first place I needed to mend. The place where I could rebuild and grow stronger.

"Your fort is damaged," she had said, "but that doesn't mean it has been defeated. Protect it and grow with it."

I thought about writing my professor a letter and telling her to take care of her fort, but the thing is, you can't protect people from their own sadness.

In the afternoon, I went to work. My first day back since the accident. I don't normally work Mondays because of school, but I didn't want to sit at home alone. The skin around my stitches has been crusty and itchy. It was so irritating that it was all I could concentrate on, so I asked Kip if I could leave. He has insisted that I take weeks off, but I don't want to. I don't like being away from Mahala. My house felt empty when I got home. There was nothing in the fridge so I went into my bedroom. I closed the blinds and switched on the fairy lights hanging above my bed. There is a tasseled rug in the middle of my floor and I laid down.

I feel strange because I don't feel sad. Things are good and I am in love with Alex. There wasn't an exact moment where I knew I was in love with her. It just happened, like the way the sun rises each morning. You never notice until the light creeps in through your window and you realize it's a new day. Over time, I have noticed things about her that I cannot go without. The way she does her hair when she dresses for work, how she has her coffee, when her confidence beams, and the look in her eyes when she is about to kiss me.

I don't remember how long I stayed on the floor, but then I heard, "You and your dad never lock the door."

I startled so much my heartbeat doubled.

Alex was in the doorway.

I said, "Hey," as casually as one can when someone scares the hell out of them.

"Are you okay?"

"I'm fine. Why aren't you at work?"

She shrugged and came into my room and laid down next to me.

"Because I wanted to see that you were okay."

She looked so good. I know that I should have said something like thanks for checking on me, but I couldn't. She just looked so good.

I went with, "My head hurts a little."

Alex was already touching me. She started at my palm and made her way up the length of my arm. My own goosebumps chased her fingers until she was touching my cheek and running them gently over my lips. I wanted Alex so badly. I always want Alex, but it's when she is touching me that I want her most.

We kissed slowly and then hard. Slowly, then hard, and

then fast, and then slow until there was nothing else but her lips and my lips, and I remember thinking that if I could breathe her in for the rest of time, I would choose to stay on the floor with her in the middle of my bedroom.

When the front door slammed and my dad called out, "Kayden I'm home," I was on top of Alex with my hand between her legs. We scrambled to untangle ourselves, and in the process, I bumped the back of my head on my bed leg.

"God damn."

Alex sighed and grabbed my face between her hands. "My thoughts exactly." She kissed me and then stood up.

"Just helping Kayden with her itchy stitches, Mr. S!" she called back, and I could hear my dad let out a roar of laughter. Alex smiled at me and said, "He really loves dad jokes."

I twisted myself so I could put my shirt on properly. My dad wouldn't have even registered that the house was quiet and both Alex and I were in my bedroom alone. It's times like these I wish I had the money to move out.

"Pizza!" he called again.

I stopped Alex in my doorway and kissed her softly. "Sleep over."

She smiled into my lips. "I stay wherever there is pizza."

Remind me to have pizza every single night from now on.

Thanks for listening,
Kayden

February 7, 2013

Dear Keeper,

Today is my birthday. I am twenty-three years old. I still feel like I am fifteen sometimes. People in my high school are married and having babies, and I am still trying to put one foot in front of the other. My therapist says this is okay. She says each person boards the train at different times. It's not about when or how soon, all that matters is getting on the train. I thought you should know that it turns out sadness does come back. I was sad this morning, because while Alex's mom wished me a happy birthday, my own mom didn't. When I got to my therapy session, I realized that sadness comes back to remind us that it's here and it's never going to truly go away. And I think this is because we need sadness to understand what happiness is.

"Balance," my therapist said when I asked her about it. "Life is just about balance."

"What happens when you fall off the balance beam?"

She said that in those times, I need to be kinder to myself and listen to my thoughts. "Be a friend to yourself, Kayden, not an enemy."

Yesterday was my last session. At least until any time I may need the sessions again. My therapist wished me happy birthday and asked what I was doing.

I said, "Celebrating—" then paused. "Celebrating one more year."

She knew what I meant, and she said I have progressed more recently than I ever had in previous years. She also said she was proud of me and that she has always had faith in me. This made me feel good. She also told me to keep writing to you, because you seem to be helping, and I told her that you have helped a great deal.

"You're stronger, Kayden," she said. "Some days you will feel stronger than other days, but on those difficult days, it doesn't mean you are any less strong or any less capable."

"Thank you," I said, because even though it had taken all this time, she had never broken her promise. She had listened to me. Before I left, I paused in the doorway and I asked her if she thought sad people were meant for this life.

She checked her watch before looking up at me and said, "Off the record?"

I smiled and said, "Sure."

"Sadness is just another word for being soft."

I didn't say anything because I didn't know what to say.

Then she said, "Soft people are needed."

"I think you're right."

"Someday you are going to need your softness, Kayden."

"When will I know?"

"You'll know."

I applied for the marine internship today. I included the reference from my professor, and Kip gave me a reference and so did my boss. If Mahala could give me a reference, I am sure she would've as well. Alex told me that she had a surprise for me for my birthday. She has been teasing me about it all day because I want to know what it is. As it happens, I heard the front door close three minutes ago, and now Alex is standing in my bedroom doorway in lacy underwear.

This is going to be a very good birthday. Perhaps the best one yet.

Thanks for listening,
Kayden

February 14, 2013

Dear Keeper,

It's Valentine's Day.

I want to do something for Alex even though she has only been my official girlfriend for a month. When I asked my dad for ideas, he said Valentine's Day is a waste of time and money. This might be true because you don't need just one day to tell someone you love them, but maybe some people do. Then he saw the look on my face and told me that whatever I decided to do, Alex would like it.

"But I want to show her, Dad."

He laughed and said, "I think she knows."

"No, but I want her to *really* know."

He thought while he drank his coffee.

Then he said, "The reason I first fell in love with your mom is because I could be myself around her."

"What changed?"

He looked at me the same way he always does when I ask about him and Mom. Like the memories still pain him.

"I couldn't be myself anymore."

"So how does this help me with Alex?"

"Take her somewhere that you love the most. Share it with her."

"Is that what happened with you and Mom?you couldn't share things anymore?"

He ran his mug under the faucet and stood there watching the water as it swirled and spilled over the edges of the rim. "I think when you stop sharing things, you lose yourself. And I think all anyone wants is to be found."

I thought about how I had stopped sharing my secrets until I was told to write them down. I thought about how Alex had found me at a very strange time and she hadn't told me to be quiet. She had told me to speak.

I said, "I love you, Dad."

"Love you too, kid." And he hugged me, because even though he didn't believe in Valentine's Day, I knew that somewhere under all the grease in his fingernails, he still believed in someone finding him.

When I went to work, I found Kip and explained that I wanted to do something nice for Alex. He said I should buy her a giant teddy bear, but I told him I didn't want to do that.

"Can I borrow the Marine Center?"

Kip looked at me as though he hadn't heard me properly. "Try again, but with more words."

"I want to do something romantic for Alex, so I want to borrow Ray Bay tonight. It won't be long and you can stay here in case anything goes wrong."

"Why, are you going to throw her in one of the displays?"

"No, I meant if I get so nervous that I throw up."

Kip was in the middle of sorting through food for the sandbar sharks, which I was supposed to be helping with, but I didn't want to smell like fish before Alex got here.

"What time is she getting here?"

"After 8pm, when we close."

"So you're just going to sit in Ray Bay? I really think the teddy bear—"

"Kip! I am going to set it all up, just promise you'll help me. This is important."

I saw his eyes drift to the thin white scar on the top of my forehead and then to my eyes and back to the scar again.

"Well, go take the front desk for the afternoon. No use in you smelling worse than penguin shit when she gets here."

I hugged him so hard the bucket was knocked from his hand.

"Front desk!"

"I'm gone, I'm gone."

I couldn't think of anything else other than Alex. I explained to Laura (the girl on front desk today; she's been here two months) what I was going to do. I didn't stop myself when I spoke about Alex as my girlfriend, and Laura didn't seem to get awkward or anything. She just listened and nodded a lot and gave me some more ideas. When things started winding down and the customers filed out until there was no one left in the Center other than a handful of keepers and employees, I felt even more nervous.

Kip found me as I was shuffling through the notes I had written.

"Table is set with chairs. Lights are low but the tank is shining. No fire allowed but I did get a fake candle with batteries during my lunch break."

He was grinning at me, but he looked confused when he saw I wasn't smiling.

"What's wrong?"

"I'm scared again."

"About what?"

"What if she doesn't love me back?"

Kip sighed and said, "Kayden, you're not going to know everything that's going to happen in your life. You didn't know Alex was going to write back to your letter, you didn't know that you were going to crash your car, you don't know if you are going to get into the marine program. You don't have to know everything, you just have to live. You're going to be disappointed sometimes, but you're also going to find that other things work out."

"You sound like my therapist."

"Really? I should start charging."

He made me laugh.

"You feel good? Alex makes you feel like there are no more holes and secrets?"

"Yes."

He reached for my shoulders and placed a big brown hand on either side, "Then live, Kayden. Live while you can."

I love Kip. Truly. There have been moments where I have cried to my therapist about how I could be so sad when I have people around me who won't let me float away. She said it was because sometimes we cannot hear the ocean even if we are standing in front of it. Instead we have to find a shell and place it to our ear.

Before Alex arrived, I messed up all the notes because I was so nervous. Then Jupiter escaped yet again and I had to call Kip to help me put him back in the tank. Kip thought the whole thing was funny. I could tell he was enjoying himself. He helped me place the notes properly and adjusted the lighting for me around Ray Bay. He had set up a table and two chairs and put out the silverware and the plates and I hoped the Italian food I'd bought from across the road would be okay. Then I picked out music to play on the overhead speakers. I think I did alright but I was still anxious because I wanted Alex to like it. Then she texted me and told me she was outside.

"Kip, go hide in the office."

"Got it, Rayden. Good luck!"

I texted Alex back and told her to follow the notes. I will write down what each of them said.

1. *From guest services, turn around and find the next note at the rock pools.*

2. *When I'm with you, I don't have to be anyone else, I can just be me. Go right, past the clown fish and the coral reef exhibit and find the next note on the jellyfish display.*

3. *Go through the Lost City of Atlantis and find the next note on our shark shipwreck exhibit.*

4. *You make me laugh and you make me the happiest I have ever been. Turn left at the submarine simulator, pick up the next note taped to the window.*

5. *Go out onto the riverfront exhibit and then left past the otter house, collecting the last note on the way.*

6. *I know that I have been afraid and scared and running from us, but I don't want to anymore. I want to always share everything with you. Follow the path and find me in Ray Bay – K*

When Alex found me in Ray Bay, she had a smile on her face that I will never forget. Like she felt wanted. I want her to always feel wanted. She was wearing a black dress and it hung from her shoulders and her hips the way a breeze does in the trees. She had curled her hair and it fell across her shoulders like waves do when they wash up on the sand. Her eyes looked a brighter green than usual, and her freckles stood out even in the shadows. I could spend days writing down all the words that came to my mind in that moment. That I was falling more in love with her, that my heart sighed every time I saw her, that I wanted to be with her wherever she was. She was so beautiful. I know that Alex is much more than that. I know that she is smart and funny and likes to tease the people closest to her. But when you are standing in front of a woman and your heart is in your throat, you just want to pull all these words together into one. Then I noticed that she was carrying a white rose. When Alex handed this to me, for the first time in all the time I had known her, she looked nervous. We managed to settle into the table and I poured soda I had bought from the vending machine into cups and dished spaghetti onto her plate.

Alex had a small smile on her face when she said, "I didn't know you could be so romantic."

I said, "I hope the food is okay."

"I'm just really impressed we're eating Italian and not what you feed Mahala."

I kicked her leg under the table in response.

"To us," Alex said, holding her cup to mine, "and to you, for loving fish so much."

I almost spit out the soda, almost.

When I was with Shaye, I wanted people to like us together. I wanted to tell everyone that I was gay and I wanted them to be happy about it. Now I realize that not everyone is going to be happy about it. But even if they stare, they'll never know the love I have for Alex. She is the sun and I am the sky, she is the mountain and I am the snow, she is the shore and I am the ocean. My heart no longer feels heavy, but full. I know that there will be struggles, but I will struggle if it means I can struggle with her. I want Alex, the good parts and the bad parts. I want her to know that every part of her makes me want to be better than I was before. I want her to know that I love how my name sounds in her mouth, how her laugh makes me think of music, and that even if this love makes our lives harder, I would live a harder life just so I could be with her. I had been so busy staring at her that when she asked me if I recognized the song playing above us, it took me a moment to realize what she was talking about.

"This was the song playing when we first kissed," she said.

Then Alex leaned across the table, and she had the same fire in her eyes that she did the night we had mimosas, and she whispered, "Dance with me."

I could feel her body against mine, her arms wrapped around my neck and my hands on her hips as we moved slowly and probably out of time, but it didn't matter because it felt like we were floating. Her nose was against mine and her breath was on my lips and her eyes were so close I could see every speck of green. I told Alex that I feel like I am an ocean and that she is my harbor. Every time I am pulled away in my thoughts, I know that I will return to her. The rays knew something was happening, because they weren't hiding, they were swimming as close to our side of the glass as possible, and I could tell Mahala was watching us. Bright light splayed over the walls in fluorescent blue. It felt like we were suspended in an ocean of our own.

Then Alex whispered, "I love you."

"I love you, too."

Her head tilted and our lips met to the close the space between us. I felt her hands in my hair as she gripped the back of my neck and pulled us closer.

I love Alex like she makes the earth rotate.

It's Valentine's Day and I hope you have someone who will call you beautiful when you need to hear it most. Even if you don't, I hope you know that you are.

Thanks for listening,
Kayden

February 22, 2013

Dear Keeper,

When the sun rises, its light reaches my bedroom window first. It falls in between the drapes and touches all that it can. In the middle of the night, we had pulled the sheet over our heads, so this morning when I woke up, the first thing I saw was Alex, asleep under a sea of cream. I had forgotten what being in love feels like. That feeling in my stomach where I wanted to watch her for hours. I wanted to watch her lips, how they are soft and pink and parted slightly when she sleeps. Her body was held together in a small silk nightgown and I wanted to reach over and touch her skin. And then her eyes fluttered open, those big eyes that change color depending on the day. She saw me watching her and laughed as she pulled the sheet away.

"Hi."

"Hi."

All my life, I have imagined myself to be very plain. I am soft and quiet and I get too emotional. But today Alex told me I was the most beautiful girl in the world to her. Before Alex, I didn't think I would love someone again. Love seemed dangerous. It seemed like madness to someone with so many thoughts. But the way she looks at me makes my whole life start dancing to a song that only we can hear.

Neither of us had work today so we spent the morning between the sheets. We ate toast in bed and laughed when peanut butter dribbled on our chins. And then we took off each other's clothes and explored places that made Alex's head tilt back and kiss me harder. And then we just laid there, looking at each other.

Alex said, "Let's not leave this bed."

"Okay."

I have never been naked in the way I am naked with Alex. She sees parts of me that I am not even sure I see myself.

Alex said, "I'm really proud of you."

"Why?"

"Because you're still here."

She was tracing circles across the top of my hand and I was watching her, thinking about how glad I was that I had written everything down in the last few months.

"Writing has helped." I said.

She nodded, "I did the same thing when Dad left us."

I turned towards her, moving my arm so it laid across her stomach. "Do you think if I had started writing earlier, maybe I would have felt better earlier?"

Alex's lips curled into a smile, and she brushed my hair behind my ears, "There's no timeframe, Kayden. It's not like you take some antibiotics and your cold goes away in a week or so."

I thought about this, "I think I just wanted somebody to notice I was still here. That I hadn't left."

Alex shook her head, "Everybody always feels sorry for the person who leaves. But when all the dust settles, nobody ever talks about the people they leave behind. That's what my mom said at my lowest point."

"Does yours stay with you?"

"My sadness?"

"Yeah."

She nodded, "Always. But it doesn't feel as bad. Sometimes when I can't feel it, I almost miss it."

Alex brought her hand to my face, rubbing my cheek with her thumb. I could see the tattoo on her wrist so clearly in the lighting from my window.

I had asked Alex about her favorite color, her favorite film, and her favorite song. I had asked her where she went to school and if she liked the taste of chocolate mint. But even though I loved her tattoo, I had never asked her what it meant. So I reached for her wrist and asked, "What does it mean?"

She looked at it and said, "It was in my dad's suicide note."

I didn't let go of her wrist, I just traced my thumb over each letter, 엄마 잘돌봐 continuously.

"Why is it in Korean?"

She didn't say anything for a while but then she said, "The only family holiday we ever had together was to Busan in South Korea. My dad was there for a work conference. He had taken a day off to bring me hiking through the

174

mountains. I didn't think anything of it, but he told me to always remember our trip to Busan if I needed him. I just liked the way the writing looked."

"It's beautiful."

Alex didn't take her eyes off me, and I could feel them, like they were burning through my skin. If she were watching me from hundreds of yards away, I know I would still feel her gaze.

"It means 'Take care of your mom.'"

"I like that."

Alex moved and settled her body between my legs. Her skin was warm and her breathing deepened with every kiss.

"I love you," she whispered, and it filled the room.

It must have been early evening, because the front door closed and I heard my dad call out, "Chinese!"

I think he does this even when I'm not home.

Alex was sleeping so I whispered, "Wake up," in her ear and she stirred from where her face had been buried against my neck.

Then Alex's phone lit up with a text message. I reached for it to pass it to her, but I noticed that it was Brandon texting and I felt my stomach knot. She was half asleep but I think she felt my body tense.

She asked, "What?" groggily.

"Nothing, I didn't see anything."

"I know when you're lying, Kayden."

She fiddled with her phone and read the text message. She looked confused for a moment, then annoyed, and then finally she sighed.

"I need to tell you something."

"What is it?"

"Brandon is moving back to East Point."

This was not the news I was expecting.

"Okay."

"But I want you to know that it's not going to get in the way of us."

"Alex, usually when people say things like this, it means that it will."

"This is different."

I don't really want him to move back.

Thanks for listening,
Kayden

March 10, 2013

Dear Keeper,

I am trying to write as often as I can, but I have been so busy with papers and preparing for exams. Do you remember last week when I told you that Alex's ex-boyfriend is moving back to Long Island? Well he's here. Do you also remember when I told you back in December how Kip said there was going to be a new otter handler at the Marine Center? It's him. I cannot believe all those months back when Kip told me a new keeper was transferring in the new year that it was going to be Alex's ex-boyfriend Brandon. I didn't even know he worked in marine biology. He's going

176

to ruin this. I'm having all these thoughts because I'm probably jealous, at least that's what Joe says. But the Marine Center is where I feel safe. Now he's strutting around introducing himself to everyone as "the new guy" and I have been awkwardly trying to avoid him. I don't even think he knows Alex is dating again. And I definitely don't want to know what he is going to think when he finds out Alex is dating a girl. I don't even have time to think about all these things because I am too anxious about the results of the marine program and the internship.

On Brandon's first day, all the girls said he was cute.

Laura said to me, "You can appreciate attractive men, though, right?"

I smiled and nodded instead of saying what I wanted to say, which would have been something like, "Maybe I'd appreciate him more if he weren't my girlfriend's ex."

I avoided the otter house all day. When I got home, I called Nate and he came over for dinner. We sat on my bedroom floor eating fried rice and dumplings from Mr. Koi's.

Nate isn't very good at using chopsticks, but he tries.

"Bit weird he's back. Who is this guy?"

"Her ex."

He grinned and said, "I got that part, I meant what's his story?"

"I don't know, Alex tries not to talk about him."

"Shit must have happened."

"What do you mean?"

"I mean he must have hurt her real bad."

"I can't stand him."

Nate laughed and fried rice sprayed all over my floor. "Man, you love this girl."

"Of course I do, and now her ex is working at the same place I do, and I don't know anything about him other than Laura Henderson thinks he's cute."

"The fuck is Laura Henderson?"

I groaned and said, "Can you just tell me what to do?"

"Well you trust Alex, right?"

"Yes."

"Then don't worry about it, Peanut. Besides, if he tries anything, I'll kick his ass."

I fiddled with my dumplings to the point that I had smashed them all together and I didn't feel like eating them anymore.

"What is it when you trust the person you're with but not the people around her?"

"Fear."

There it was again.

On Brandon's second day, I avoided him by sorting mysids (they're small shrimp we feed to leafy seadragons) and hiding out near the freezers. Kip asked if I was okay because I was acting strange and I told him I had my period. He was awkward for a few moments but then he left me alone all day. Then in the evening I called Joe and asked if jealously can drive people crazy.

"Yes."

"How do I know if I'm jealous?"

"Do you hate this guy?"

"No, I just don't trust him."

"Why?"

"Because he seems fake."

"Maybe he is fake."

"But how would I tell?"

"Something will probably happen."

"Are you and Nate okay?"

"Do we seem okay?"

"Not really."

"Yeah."

"Joe?"

"Yeah?"

"I'm sorry."

"It's not your fault, Kayden. I'm glad you're happy with Alex."

"You won't be sad forever."

"I know."

Today I managed to keep my distance from Brandon for a few hours, but I accidentally ran into him in the staff room.

He said, "Kayden, right?"

"That's me."

I hardly stayed long enough for him to finish asking me if the sodas in the vending machine were free. I snuck out and told Laura I would take over the photography on front door. She looked at me like she had to trade something for it, but I told her I was in an extra good mood and wanted to greet our customers. This was a complete lie, I never want to talk to anyone unless I have to, but I needed to hide out somewhere that I knew Brandon wasn't going to be. When

I got off work, I caught the bus to Alex's house.

She has been on edge all week about Brandon and I working together.

"Did he speak to you today?"

I replied, "No. Maybe once in the lunch room, but I can't remember."

"What did he say?"

She sounded upset, like she really wanted to know if he had said something to me.

"Just if the sodas in the vending machine were free. Which they are if you swipe your employee card, but I forgot to tell—"

"Did you tell him who you were?"

"No." She made me feel anxious, so I asked, "Why are you making such a big deal about this?"

"Because he's my ex and I don't want him knowing about us."

"Why?"

"Because I just don't."

"Who cares? You're not with him anymore, you're with me."

"You don't understand."

That hurt.

"I'm trying to."

She sighed and said, "Just forget I said anything, okay? Morgan needs a lift from the station, do you want to come?"

"I think I am just going to walk home."

Alex looked at me as if I had offended her for wanting to leave and it made my stomach turn over about a thousand times.

She whispered, "Fine, I'll see you tomorrow."

She left me in her room and she didn't call back 'I love you' over her shoulder like she usually does.

Thanks for listening,
Kayden

March 14, 2013

Mahala died yesterday. I can't talk about it just yet.

March 20, 2013

Dear Keeper,

I am sorry about the last time I wrote to you. I was upset and I couldn't find any words. I was crying so much I could barely see what I was writing. Today I am doing better I think. Mahala got sick. The ray keepers said it could have been several things but mostly put it down to age. I found her that morning as I walked in for work. Kip was right behind me and he called the keepers because I couldn't speak. But I knew she was gone.

Kip dropped by this afternoon. He brought me a framed picture of Mahala and I in the tank from a few months back. Kip had been trying to take a photo when I was cleaning the inside of the tank, and Mahala came right up behind me. I remember the brief panic in Kip's eyes because of her size compared to mine. Her wingspan could engulf me. But he calmed down after a moment because Mahala wasn't a threat to me. I hadn't finished cleaning the filter so I kept working on it and Mahala stayed beside me. It was the last time I was in the water with her. Part of me wonders if perhaps she was saying goodbye. The Center is having a memorial, which they don't normally do. We rescue animals all the time but some don't survive due to their injuries. It's just the way of life; we die and another is born. But I think they are holding the memorial on my account and also because Mahala was our first manta ray. Kip asked me if I was okay about fifteen times this afternoon. I had to make him a cup of tea just so he would stop looking at me as though I was going to crumble again. I told him I am different from how I was back then. Because I am. Even my grief feels different. It's bearable. It's like even though the pain will always be there, you wake up every morning knowing you can survive it.

Even so, the memorial is tomorrow and I will probably cry.

Thanks for listening,
Kayden

March 21, 2013

Dear Keeper,

Spring is here. The days are warmer and the flowers are opening. The air smells like lavender during the day and pine oak at night time. Kip made a small headstone at the back of the Center near some trees that are scattered down to the marina. Mahala obviously won't be buried here. They sometimes take the animals for research purposes or return them to the ocean to feed another circle of life. But I don't want to think about that because it makes me sad. The headstone says, "Mahala, a good friend." I sat there for a long time today and I told Mahala how much I was going to miss her. And I cried, because death reminds me of many things I have felt, and it makes me think about Shaye. Triggers are not cured, as some people think. You cannot wake up one day and suddenly the thing that was very traumatic in your life is forgotten. Some people can heal from these things easier than others, but this doesn't mean they don't think about them from time to time. Mahala's death has made me think a lot about Shaye, and I wonder how she is and where she is and if she is in a better place and if she is happier than she was here on Earth. Her parents buried her in Edmonson, but then they moved away and left her. Then I left her to move to Long Island. Maybe all Shaye ever wanted was for people not to leave. But I will always wonder why she left first.

Alex texted me to see how I was and I told her that I was sitting outside on my lunch break. Then she texted back and told me that she would meet me. I curled my knees to my chest and sat back against the tree, and I thought about who I was before I started working at the Center. Even though I know that person still exists, I don't want her to come back. I like the person I am now. I like who I am with Alex.

Alex pulled up in her car and stepped out. I have all these memories of Alex now. When I think back on all the times she has been with me, I can remember what she was wearing, how she smelled, and how her skin felt against mine. We have built these memories together. Going bowling, parking out by the marina, crying in her arms because sometimes the day was too hard. I think you could spend a lifetime with someone and not remember any of the conversations you had, but you'd always remember the memories that made you feel something. She sat down next to me and took my hand. She kissed the tops of my knuckles.

"I'm sorry about Mahala."

"Me too."

"I'm sorry about a lot of things in the last few weeks."

"They're not your fault."

"I know, but I'm still sorry about them."

I nodded and looked at the headstone. "Do you think it's weird that I was so attached to a manta ray?"

Alex shook her head and squeezed my hand. "No. If you feel something and it's real to you, then nothing else matters."

I said, "I'm not good at this. The part where you have to grieve and move on. I always get stuck at the part where I have to move on. Like the sadness wants to stay and I let it."

I remember her picking up a leaf and running it along the length of my arm.

Then she said, "It's okay to be sad when people die."

"I know, but not if you stay sad forever."

"You've come a long way, Kayden. You're not who you used to be."

I thought about this and said, "I know."

"And I know sometimes you feel sad for no reason. One day you are happy and the next you aren't. But you're not alone, because sometimes I feel sad for no reason, too. It just takes time to admit it."

And then her head was on my shoulder and all I could think about was how much Alex means to me. She's outgoing and confident when she's around other people. I know this because I have watched her work at Green Leaf. She moves and people's eyes follow her. She laughs and they laugh with her. She smiles and they smile back. She says things people are too afraid to say. She walks with purpose.

But when we are alone, she's different. She is soft and she is gentle. She tells me things like it is the first time they are leaving her lips.

I said, "I know it sounds stupid, but Mahala kept me here."

"That doesn't sound stupid."

"She gave me something to live for when I felt like I shouldn't be alive."

Alex kissed my neck. "Shaye's death wasn't your fault."

"I know, but why does it feel like it was sometimes?"

"Because we feel guilty, even when we don't have to."

We sat there for a while and my lunch break was well and truly over, but Kip said I could take as long as I liked. Then Alex shifted and I knew that she wanted to tell me something because she had that look in her eye. She always has this look when she wants to talk about things that are important.

"I know that things are weird with Brandon here."

"It's not that weird, I trust you."

Alex smiled and said, "I trust you, too." Then she moved so she could sit in my lap and kiss me.

She grinned into my lips the way she always does when she wants to say something but I can't stop kissing her.

"You are never close enough."

I pulled on her dress, "So come closer."

Then she whispered, "You don't even realize how beautiful you are, Kayden."

The butterflies haven't gone away yet and I can't stop thinking about this afternoon because it has been a long time since a girl has called me beautiful and meant it. My lips are still tingling from the way she kissed me. It felt like it was just us sitting under the tree and no one else existed.

If I could live in a world with just Alex, I would do it.

Thanks for listening,
Kayden

April 10, 2013

Dear Keeper,

Yesterday was Alex's birthday. We had breakfast with Amy and Morgan at a cafe in town. Amy asked me if I had applied for the marine program in California, and I told that I had.

She said something like, "Good. I think you have a good shot considering your grades."

Morgan had two plates of food to himself and had already devoured the rest of my hash browns. He was eating Alex's when he said, "Mom is doing background checks on you."

Then Alex said, "*Morgan*," in the way sisters do when brothers are being annoying.

Amy reassured me and said, "I have done no such thing, Kayden. The program is a great opportunity, that's all."

I wanted to change the subject because I hadn't thought about what would happen if I actually got in. There were all these unanswered questions and I wasn't ready to start answering them.

The waiter came to the rescue when he delivered a bagel

to the table with a candle poking out of the middle. Morgan started singing "Happy Birthday" really loudly and Alex tried to tell him to stop singing so loudly and Amy and I looked at each other and couldn't stop laughing. It was one of those moments that I'll remember when I'm old because I felt so happy.

After breakfast, I had a surprise planned for Alex, but we needed to stop in at the Center first because Kip wanted to give Alex a gift. Everything went really well until Brandon happened to turn around the corner at the same time we were standing in the petting area talking to Kip.

"Alex!"

It wasn't the first time they had seen each other since he had been back. East Point isn't that big, so you end up running into people all the time. Alex had told me the other week that she had run into Brandon at the gym, but I was too busy studying then to worry much about it.

Alex said hello, but it was strained.

Brandon is tall, so when he stands next to me I feel like I am standing next to the Empire State Building. But Alex is the same height as me and she says she loves this because when we dance she can look into my eyes.

"I see you have been making friends with other marine fanatics, Alex."

He was referring to me.

Then Alex said, "She's not my friend."

"Well do you usually hang out with people who aren't your friends on your birthday?"

It's weird that Brandon knows things about Alex. I mean

of course he does because they were together for a year or something, but it's still strange knowing that another person knows these things about the girl I love. I wondered if Brandon knew that Alex smells the spine of every notebook she buys or that she peels the skin off peaches even though you don't need to. I wonder if he knows that in high school she wanted to die the tips of her hair blue but used the wrong hair dye so her hair turned orange.

"Kayden's my girlfriend."

"That's what I said."

In that moment, I very much wanted to jump into the rock pools and hide with the starfish.

"We're dating."

There was an awkward silence for a moment, and then Kip clapped Brandon on the back. "Kayden's got a big surprise for her lucky lady today, we'd better get back to work!"

I silently mouthed to him, "Thank you."

Kip started to leave, and then he said, "Oh, how'd the marine program go?"

"I'm still waiting to hear from them."

Brandon asked what marine program, and Kip told him I had applied for a marine program in California. Then Brandon gave me a strange look that I am still thinking about. It was like he knew exactly what program I was referring to, which he might because he has been in the marine industry a while. You have to be, to be qualified in the way he is. But it was more than that. It's like he was interested but for the wrong reasons. Like he'd had an idea.

I'm trying not to think about it; he is literally the last thing I want to be thinking about right now.

When we left the Center, I asked Alex in the car if Brandon knew she liked girls before today.

"I had mentioned it once or twice, but he chose to make fun of it."

"Ass."

Alex laughed.

Sometimes when I look at Alex, I imagine my eyes are closed and all I can see is her soul. I forget about the way her hair rises and falls in the wind or how dark her eyelashes are and how good her lips look in the sunlight. Instead I concentrate on how she makes me laugh, her resilience and strength, and the warm feeling in my stomach every time she says my name. I think about whether our souls have met before, maybe in a different lifetime. I think about keeping my eyes shut so that she will always know how much my soul loves hers. Sorry, I'm getting distracted.

Then Alex said, "He just didn't understand. But it doesn't matter anymore, because I am with someone who does."

"Was it hard?"

"What?"

"Coming out?"

She shrugged and said, "I didn't really come out. I just decided that I liked men and women and that was that. I told Mom I didn't want to be labeled. I just wanted to find a person who understood me. I didn't care about their gender."

"I like that your mom is understanding."

"Well she has exposure to all these different things on campus, you know. She's more open and she gets it."

"I know, I wish my mom would get it. I wish she would stop sending me emails about repenting."

"She does get it. She just sees it differently."

I looked out the window and watched the houses rushing past and the trees and the lines on the road blurring all together. Every person sees all things differently, but how my mom sees things affects *me*. Where do you draw the line?

"My mom and I just have a complicated relationship."

Alex reached for my hand and brought it to her lips. She kissed it softly before glancing at me and then looking back to the road. "I know. But someday if we get married and have kids, we'll teach them to be open. We get to raise a life to see all other lives as equal. There's power in that. Now where are we going?"

I was still so stuck on the part where she had talked about us getting married and having kids that I completely missed our exit. It didn't matter because I could just keep driving in Alex's old boxed beetle from here until whenever she wanted to get married.

I turned down her car radio and took out my handheld radio. The Beatles were playing.

I grinned at her and said, "You'll see."

We drove until we reached Montauk. There is a town about seven miles from the main city center. It's quiet and not many people live there, but they have a giant butterfly house. Alex loves butterflies, just like her mom. Kip told me about this spot one afternoon when I was trying to decide what to get Alex for her birthday.

191

We turned down the street on the right and I pointed to a sign that said "Butterfly House".

The car jolted forward to a stop and Alex squealed, "You didn't!

I tried not to think about the whiplash before I said, "I didn't buy you a thousand butterflies, but I did get us tickets to go hang out with a few."

She unclipped her seat belt so quickly, I didn't have time to blink before she kissed me.

Then I told her to wait, because I wanted to give her the other present. I reached into my backpack and handed her the very badly wrapped gift. I have never been very good at wrapping presents. Every Christmas my dad suggests he just wrap his own presents, and I get mad at him because I do try hard.

She said, "Kayden," softly as she unwrapped all the paper and stared at the necklace sitting inside.

Nate had helped me pick it out at the beginning of last week. It was a small silver heart with five diamonds on a silver chain. She held it out for me to clasp around her neck. I still tremble sometimes when I touch Alex. It's not because I am nervous or afraid, it's just because I didn't think I would love someone again. It makes you brave, you know? Like you can do anything.

Did you know butterflies taste with their feet? I didn't know that. I also didn't know fifty other facts about butterflies until we left for home. Alex talked about it for at least half of the drive back.

We were listening to Ben Howard when I noticed the email notification on my phone from California Marine

Hospital. When I opened the email, there were a handful of words that jumped out at me.

Congratulations, short listed, finalist.

I quickly exited my inbox, locked my phone, and put it between my legs.

"What is it?"

I lied and said, "Nothing. There's 50% off at MAC this weekend."

Alex laughed and replied, "Says the person who barely wears makeup."

I poked my tongue out at her and it wasn't long before we pulled into my driveway.

"Would you move somewhere to be with someone you loved?"

Alex turned off the engine and looked at me slowly, then she said, "I like to think I would. It depends on who the person is."

She always has this way of projecting a question back to me. She would probably make a good therapist. Although I am not sure she could sit still for so long.

"I meant if I ever moved, would you come with me?"

She looked back towards the windshield. My dad has this maple tree out front and some of the thin branches had already started to bud.

"Some people spend their whole lives wanting someone to understand them." She paused. "I know I did, before I met you."

I started to play with the hem of her dress, running my thumb along her skin and over the small birthmark on her thigh.

"So yes, I'd follow you anywhere, Kayden."

This morning when I woke up, Alex was curled next to

me with her hand locked in mine. I have been shortlisted as a finalist for the marine program. I am one step closer. Alex even hypothetically said she would follow me anywhere.

So why does it feel like I've taken a step away from her?

Thanks for listening,
Kayden

April 18, 2013

Dear Keeper,

My mom called today. This is the first time I have spoken to her this year. She ended up sending me a birthday card a month after my actual birthday. Sometimes she will also send a Christmas card but I didn't get one last year. Since I have met Alex, there are moments I wish I had a mom around. I mean, my mom is still my mom, but we don't make new memories anymore, not in the way Alex does with Amy. Then there are moments when I recognize the memories I do have. My first elementary school play, I played a flower, and Mom was in the front row. When I was twelve and I wanted to start wearing deodorant, Mom took me to the store and we tried out nearly every brand until I was satisfied, even though they all smelled the same. When I was fourteen and I cried because all the other girls at Sally Underwood's pool party were more developed than me (they probably still are), she picked me up and explained that it didn't matter what I looked like because I would always be beautiful. These are good memories. They are always fleeting. They come and then are gone as easily as they have arrived, and then they are replaced with all the ugly ones. When I was fifteen, she insisted I go on a date with Max Andrews, the pastor's son, even though I didn't want to. She would say, "Kayden, he's a nice boy, you never talk about boys!"

That summer when I wanted to wear shorts and tank tops, she insisted I wear dresses and headbands. "I feel ugly in this," I said over and over again, but she told me I would be uglier if I didn't wear the dress. After she knew I was gay, she demanded my bedroom door remain open. Once, she caught Shaye and I kissing and she tore apart my room and removed anything that she believed was "gay". But in all of this, it was never the screaming as her and Dad fell apart. It was always the quiet moments. When I would walk into the room and she would look at me and then look away.

Mom's voice sounded dry over the phone, like she had a cold.

"Kayden?"

"Mom?"

It felt weird saying that.

"Hi."

"Do you want Dad?"

"No, I called to speak to you."

"Okay."

"Mother's Day is next month."

"I'm not sure I will make it this year, I graduate soon."

"But you always come for Mother's Day, the church—"

"Yeah, well, maybe you could find a fill-in this year, Mom."

"You are my only daughter."

I hate when she says things like this.

"I understand that, but I am graduating."

"You haven't even invited me to your graduation, so the least you can do is come here for Mother's Day."

It's always about her.

"Because I don't want you at my graduation."

Silence.

"I will pay for your ticket."

She makes me so angry.

"I need to think about it."

"Why?"

I didn't need to think; I didn't even want to go.

"I'll come on one condition?"

"Yes?"

"I'm bringing my girlfriend."

I hung up because I didn't want to hear her stuttering through the phone and trying to pretend that by "girlfriend" I meant a college friend. I shouldn't have to drag out the old mask every time I go back to Colorado to see her. My mom likes to pretend a lot. She pretended that I wasn't gay. She pretended that Shaye didn't exist. Then when Shaye died, she pretended that her daughter was very upset over the loss of her *best friend*. Now she likes to pretend that her daughter is very busy away at college. But I don't have to pretend to be anyone other than myself with Alex, so I am not going to put on a façade with my mother. Not anymore.

Once in junior high, I saw the school counselor and told her my name was Ashley. She said she knew my name was Kayden and asked why I wanted her to call me something different. I told her it was because I wanted to pretend to be somebody else. If I wasn't myself, then I wouldn't be having all these feelings that I couldn't explain. If I wasn't myself, then I wouldn't cry after school, I wouldn't feel anxious in new places, and I wouldn't talk so softly that most people had to say, "What did you say?" every time I opened my mouth. She said she wasn't going to call me Ashley and that I shouldn't want to be anyone else. Then I started to cry because being me *hurt*. She told me something that has taken a long time to sink in. She said that the bravest people aren't the ones that pretend they're fine when they're not. It's the ones that admit they aren't fine but carry on anyway. I just want my mom to tell me she is afraid. I want her to tell me that she understands but she doesn't know how to act. I don't want her to keep pretending that I'm some Ashley and not Kayden.

I decided to go for a run in the afternoon because my thoughts were throbbing in my head and I felt anxious. When I got home, Dad had invited Nate, Joe, and Tyler over to watch the New York Lizards game. I walked into the living room and Alex was sitting between Joe and Nate holding a bowl of Doritos as though she was born to be a chip stand. I knew that she had purposely sat between them because she was trying to make things less awkward, and I loved her for that.

My dad asked, "Good run?"

"Yes. Did you know the Andrews have a baby now?"

My dad grinned and said the baby had more hair than him, and I rolled my eyes.

"I need to take a shower."

Joe said, "That's your cue, Alex."

Nate laughed, while my dad and Alex went bright red. Then he high fived Joe and it wasn't a pretend high five. It was the same laugh Nate always does whenever Joe says something funny. It was something so small, but I knew it was good for them. Like they were Nate and Joe again.

It sounds like a bowl just got knocked over downstairs, and I wonder if Joe jumped up too quickly and spilled the Doritos all over my girlfriend. I can hear Nate hollering at the TV and Tyler telling him to shut up. I even just heard my dad offer Alex a beer. I wish you could come over and watch the game with us. It's nice to be with people who don't pretend.

Just promise me you won't pretend to be something that you're not, okay?

Thanks for listening,
Kayden

May 9, 2013

Dear Keeper,

When I asked Alex if she would come to Colorado with me, she had this look in her eye as if to say she would enjoy the challenge. I told her she didn't have to come because it was Mother's Day and wouldn't she want to spend it with Amy, but she said she would just take Amy out next week. She told me she knew how hard this was for me but that I didn't have to be alone anymore and that I had her. You meet someone and after all the small talk and the awkward glances and the debate that happens in your brain about whether you should hold their hand or not, suddenly you are talking about their scars and their bruises and the moments that have made them cry and the moments that have made them laugh until their stomach hurts. Alex calls me when I am half asleep because she can't sleep without me. I can talk for hours about the ocean and Alex won't take her eyes off me. When I am sad, she tells me to share. When I am angry, she listens. When I am happy, she says she loves it when I smile.

Most times that I have flown back to see my mom on Mother's Day, I haven't wanted to. We argue the entire time. I never leave the house even if she begs me to because I know that the town will whisper. Everything about Edmonson reminds me of Shaye and all the suffering we went through. That pain doesn't just disappear. It moves over and makes room for other things, but it always stays with you. In my freshman year of college, I met a girl in my biology class who didn't have a mother. At least not one that was alive. So I kept going back to my own mother. Not for any other reason, other than that somewhere underneath all the suffering, I still love my mom. But last Mother's Day, she told me to stop kissing girls. We had been to church and she had organized the lunch afterward. I'd sat in the hall and listened as all the women spoke about their daughters and their daughters' boyfriends. Then we had gone back to the house and she had told me it wasn't right to kiss girls. She said it hurt her, and that God had told her this wasn't the path he had wanted for me. To my knowledge, my mother has never physically met God. I've never physically met him either, so I was unsure where she came up with the whole path concept. I'd assumed it was one of the other women on the committee. They were always giving her these grand ideas about how to act if your child was gay. The thing is, my mother was always so busy trying to control my path, she didn't look up to see where her *own* path was going. If only she had stopped, maybe she would have noticed that as time went on, her path moved further and further away from mine.

For the record, I didn't think I would ever fall in love. I had this weird voice holding me back, talking to me in the middle of the night, and telling me that if I were to fall in love, it would bring madness and confusion and pain. So for a long time I fought myself. My heart was at war with my head. But you can't fight it for very long, because you meet someone and they remind you why it's all worth it. And now I can't stop kissing Alex, because Alex isn't small talk or awkward glances. Alex is the conversation you have late at night about why you're still fighting to be you in this world.

Our flight leaves early tomorrow morning. Alex is currently trying to teach my dad how to make homemade donuts, but all I can smell is burned dough. I am in my bedroom with clothes strewn all over the bed because I don't know what to pack. My mother always wants me to wear sun dresses and silky underwear, but all I have are tank tops and denim and men's boxer briefs. I can hear Alex laughing and I can hear my dad swearing. I wish my mom loved Alex as much as my dad does. I wish my mom were more like Amy. But she's not. In the spirit of all the sharing I have been doing over the last few months, I am not going to lie to you. I'm petrified. I don't know how my mom is going to react, I don't know what she is going to say, and I don't know how I am going to handle myself. I have been doing so well. I don't want to shut down again. But I can't go back to Edmonson without Alex. I can't go back alone.

Thanks for listening,
Kayden

May 10, 2013

Dear Keeper,

My mom picked us up from the airport in the early afternoon. Her hair is shorter and she looks older. She hugged me when I walked from the gate. It was a tight hug, like she wasn't going to let go. I can't remember the last time my mother has hugged me like this. She even hugged Alex, which I wasn't prepared for. Neither was Alex, because the way I have described my mother is the equivalent of a giant, Bible-wielding dragon, so when she folded her into a hug, Alex looked at me from over my mother's shoulder with this blank expression, as if she wasn't sure what she should do.

Mom also talked a lot in the car, but I wasn't listening. I was glad Alex made conversation; I was too busy staring out the window at the street names passing by in a flurry. Edmonson has not changed much. It's this dusty little town where the light still makes the mountains look like they are the backdrop of a painting and the valley still smells like firewood. The houses aren't on top of each other out here, they are more spread out, but there aren't any fences like there are in East Point. It has such crisp clean air, but every time I come back, I feel like I can't breathe. Mom's house even felt different when we arrived. She had planted pink roses along the hedge line and painted the window boxes blue. Alex commented that it was a beautiful house and my mother said she appreciated the comment. When we were inside, I knew my mother was watching. I could feel it. Every time I absently reached for Alex and then stopped and returned my hand to my pockets. It shouldn't be like this, so strained that I'm the one that feels out of place.

Alex wanted to go for a walk before dinner. She said the mountains were pretty and she wanted to see more of Edmonson. I didn't want to go out in case I came across someone I used to know. I am not sure if people ever leave small towns. I left with the intention of never coming back. Yet here I am, and I'm still just as afraid as when I left.

She whispered, "Please?" in my ear as we were making the bed in my old bedroom. My mother had promised me we could stay in the same room on the account that I had promised to make the trip. It was a fair deal. The spare bedroom was converted into a Bible reading room and I didn't think Alex would want to stay in there.

"But what if someone sees us?"

"I'll tell them I'm cousin Barbara from Iowa."

I scrunched up my nose and repeated, "Cousin Barbara from Iowa," to the point Alex laughed and wrapped her arms around my neck.

"Please let's go for a walk. It's so nice out and I want to hold your hand without your mom watching."

"Okay," I finally said, because Alex still gives me butterflies.

There is an old water tank out by Mr. Gregor's farm. At least it was his farm six years ago. The tank used to pump water into most of the businesses in town before the government came in, shut it down, and introduced irrigation systems. It's still standing, though. They left it up looking over Edmonson like a beacon in the night.

Alex immediately went for the ladder.

"You can't climb up there."

"Why not?"

"Because it's old."

She laughed and said, "So?" before she climbed all the way to the top and then I had to climb after her.

We sat on the edge and dangled our feet out over the side. If you squint up there, you can pretend you are a bird and your feet are hovering over the farm.

Alex asked if we were trespassing, and I said probably, but that it didn't matter.

"Would you ever live in a town like this?"

"No."

"I don't mean Edmonson. I mean like somewhere in the mountains."

"It depends."

"On what?"

"If you'd be there too."

She laughed, "Well, where else would I be?"

I ran my fingers along the metal frame, tapping so the sounds echoed into the late afternoon.

"I love you more than anything, Alex."

She reached for my hand, pulling it into her lap. "Breathe," she whispered.

I took a deep breath, in and out, exhaling into the coolness of the air. I trained my eyes on Alex, smiling slightly because she was looking at me like she always does, with a gentle ease that calms me.

Then she said, "I think your mom will listen to you this time."

"Hardly."

"No, I think she will. It's different, she can see that you can be normal even though you are in a relationship with a female."

"I know, but she could see I was in a relationship with Shaye and she decided to pretend I wasn't."

"My mom used to pretend that Brandon and I weren't in a relationship, too."

"Really?"

Alex nodded and looked out at the view for a moment.

Then she said, "He used to tell me that all the feelings I was having were crazy and due to my own insecurities. So I started to think that the only way to get his attention was to be confident and out there. I started acting differently and my mom noticed."

"But I love the way you are."

She always smiles when I say things like that. I don't even mean to, they just come out, but I like the way she looks when I say them.

"I just mean that I couldn't be myself with him. Not in the way I am with you. So my mom chose to pretend that he wasn't in my life. Maybe your mom pretended Shaye wasn't in your life because she knew how sad she was. Maybe she was just trying to protect you."

I had never thought about it like that.

"I want her to see you as my girlfriend, not my friend. You are more than just a friend to me."

"She will. Just give it some time."

I thought six years was plenty of time, but maybe some people aren't measured in years, they're measured in moments.

By the time we returned to the house, my mother was cooking. The sun had faded and sunk below the mountain, the last rays outlining its shape. Alex went upstairs to wash up before dinner, which left me alone with Mom for the first time since we landed. Even being in the same room together was difficult. She tried making small talk at first. She said things like, "How was your walk?" "Do you think your friend likes Edmonson?" "Can you please pass me those tomatoes?"

But my mother says more with her eyes than her voice. The way she has looked at Alex and I all day. I wonder if she is still hoping that one day I will wake up and not be this way.

"I kiss girls, Mom," I told her as she was hunched over the kitchen counter. She had been peeling potatoes at such a rate I thought she was going to peel them into nothing.

"I know."

"Then why do you keep calling Alex my friend?"

She didn't look at me.

"Because it's hard for me, Kayden."

"Hard for you?"

She looked at me as though she was tired, like she wanted me to understand her. I wanted her to realize that's all I wanted from her, too.

"I still live here," she said. "I still live in this town and have to see all these people who know you are gay. How do you think that makes me look in front of the church?"

It was always about my mother. Never about me. It took me a long time to realize that maybe it wasn't even about me being gay. Maybe it was just about how my mother was going to look to everyone else. I've never understood why something so central to my life that involves my feelings, my heart, my mind, could be so difficult for her. And in that moment, something my therapist had said suddenly dawned on me. That the pain I carry inside was not mine to carry. Shaye's pain wasn't mine to carry. My mother's resentment and the exasperation on her face every time we've had these conversations over the years is not mine to carry. It is hers.

"I can't carry this anymore, Mom."

She stopped peeling.

"This is not about you anymore, this about me. About what I want and what I need. I need Alex, and that's not going to change."

Then I told her we'd take a plate and eat it on the balcony. When I walked through the living room, I noticed she had set the table there. In the center were lilies, Alex's favorite flower. I don't know if it was coincidence or if my mother knew, but the pain was too much, and I had to look away.

Now Alex is asleep in my old bed and I am sitting against my old bedroom door. There have never been locks in this house. My mom used to say it was because God would never shut his children out, so his children shouldn't shut out their parents. I am pushing so hard against the slates I can feel them leaving imprints in my back. I have tried all my life to let my mother in, but if she comes in, she leaves a mess. This time I just want her to stay locked out.

Thanks for listening,
Kayden

May 11, 2013

Dear Keeper,

Last night after I finished writing to you, I crawled into bed with Alex. She's a light sleeper and she woke up as I wrapped my arm over her waist.

She whispered, "How is your mom?" through the dark.

I said. "Not so good," as I grazed her side. She was so warm.

Then Alex moved slightly to switch on the light. It dimly filled the room and cast shadows across the wall. It was strange that the shadows were the same shadows on my walls when I lived here years ago. Like the furniture hadn't moved and I had gone back in time. Only I was someone different.

I leaned over to kiss her, but she didn't kiss me back.

"What's wrong?"

"You haven't said anything about what we talked about yesterday."

"What is there to say?"

"You don't think I am a train wreck?"

I smiled and said, "I think if anyone is the train wreck, it's me."

"I was a different person a few years ago."

"So was I. In most ways, I'm still recovering."

"I've been with a lot of girls, Kayden," Alex said, "and guys."

"So?" I asked and I just wanted to kiss her.

"You don't think that makes me a slut?"

I struggled to reason why or how that could possibly

make her a slut and I didn't know what to say.

"I just wanted to feel something after Brandon, because he made me feel so small," she whispered. "I wanted to feel something other than emptiness."

"That doesn't make you a slut," I replied. I knew what emptiness felt like, and it was the reason why I wanted to feel sadness, to feel pain, because it was better than feeling nothing.

Alex traced her thumb over my lip and said, "When you look at me, all the emptiness goes away, and you haven't even touched me."

I've been thinking about that a lot; that we are never aware of the effect we have on other people, only the effect that they have on us. In that moment, I could see how much Alex needed me, and when you are needed by someone, it gives you a purpose for something beyond yourself.

Then she said, "Crawl inside me. To the place I am most damaged."

"Alex…"

"Find me there. Because that is where I need you to love me."

I'd never seen her vulnerable like this, and it made me want to always protect her, to keep her safe from people like my mom who didn't understand that a woman could protect another woman in the same way a man could.

I held her until we both fell asleep.

Today, I waited for Mom to go to church before we left my bedroom. There was a note on the kitchen counter that said 'Fruit in the fridge, oats in the cupboard. Be back this afternoon. Love Mom xx'.

"She loves you," Alex said over my shoulder.

"She loves who she thinks I can be, not who I am."

After breakfast, Alex wanted to meet Shaye. It took me a moment to process what she had suggested we do, and then she asked if we could walk there. I said yes, and we walked to the Edmonson graveyard. We sat at Shaye's grave for a long time and I told her about my life and that I was sorry for leaving. And then I introduced her to Alex and told her that she made me happy. Then Alex said hello and that it was nice to finally meet her and that she would do her best to take care of me. I think I fell in love with Alex more today, if that's even possible. Most people would think going to a graveyard was super weird, let alone the grave of your girlfriend's ex. But Alex didn't think it was weird, and even if she did, she didn't let on about it.

"I love you," she said as we walked back to the house. "I would do anything for you."

And I said, "I know."

"Do you?"

"Yes."

"Anything at all," she said again. "I hope you never forget that."

I nodded and squeezed her hand because I felt very loved in that moment, and I didn't want to cry because Alex might think I was crying about Shaye when I was really crying about how much Alex loved me. I love her just the same.

She is so good to me, and not because she does nice things for me or listens to me, but because she reminds me so much of what life is meant to be about: sharing.

"You make me happy," I told her as we reached my mom's mailbox.

I could tell she was trying to act cool, because that's how Alex is.

"I hope you never forget that."

Thanks for listening,
Kayden

May 12, 2013

Dear Keeper,

I need to get this all out because you won't believe what happened. Let me tell you every detail while I remember, I don't want to leave anything out.

We went to church this morning. When I told Alex that my mother was going and it was something we did on Mother's Day and that she wanted us both to come, she looked at me as though I had asked her to skydive.

"Have you ever been to church?"

"Not really," she said. "My parents aren't very religious."

"This church has pretty windows."

Then Alex asked, "Kayden, why do you want to go somewhere that hurt you? Those people punished you."

"Not all of them. And besides, I'm hoping people might change their minds if they're not so scared."

Edmonson Church has been in town for decades. It is big and white and has giant stained glass windows on either side.

As we entered, there was this familiar hymn playing. Janet Hicks still plays the organ, even after all these years. My mother sits right at the front because she usually reads a sermon. She was in front of Alex and I as we walked in, and she ushered us to the front pew. When we took our seats, I could feel the hairs on my neck standing on end because people were looking at me. I have changed since I was in high school, but I knew people recognized me. As the service started and the pastor began to talk, I became distracted with the glass windows. I like the colors, and I like the way Mary looks at Jesus. Even after everything that changes in the world and all the differences people have, a mother always loves her child. It's something nice to think about.

Alex isn't afraid to be who she is and this is one of the reasons why I love her so much. She moved her hand from her lap and she placed it neatly on my thigh, just long enough so that I would place my hand over the top and thread my fingers through hers. We were joined together, here under the pretty stained glass windows, and I felt strong, like I could stand up to anyone with Alex. It turned out I wasn't the one who was going to be standing up.

It was my mother.

I am used to my mother giving sermons or reading from the Bible because I would listen to her every Sunday. But when the pastor said, "And now a special message from Sally to her daughter, Kayden, who has joined us with her partner, Alex, for Mother's Day." I instinctively believed I had dreamed up what he had said. But I didn't dream. It happened, and I remember everything. When Mom stood up and walked to the front aisle, I could see her hands trembling. When she opened the paper and began to talk, her voice was trembling too. But she didn't stop. Not for a second. She read the whole letter.

"As most of you know, I have been on the Church Committee most of my adult life. I attended Sunday School as a child, I was married in this church, and now I run Sunday School. I sing in the choir, I teach Bible studies over the holidays, and I practice Christian principles as all of you do. Years ago, my daughter told me that she was gay. All I could think about were my own fears. I hoped that she would not walk away from God. I was afraid of what my fellow Christians would think, say, and feel, and I was afraid that her life would become a struggle. But I have recently learned that I was a large part of that struggle. Recently, something new has been born inside me. Being so blinded by what I thought was right, I failed to see that my daughter has grown into a woman who loves with her whole heart, just as God loves with his whole heart. And because my daughter is gay, she has made me do something I in turn never thought I would do. She has made me face my fears." She paused a few moments after that part, and she looked at me and for the first time in most of my life, she didn't look away.

"And so," she said, and her eyes started to water, "I am going to learn to accept my daughter, to not judge her. And I hope, as a congregation where we love one another, that we might all try to do this for all other people just like my daughter."

It wasn't like everyone stood up and started clapping. That only happens in the movies. But someone did say "Amen," and then another person said it, and another and another, until it felt like the whole congregation had agreed with my mom. I doubt the entire church agreed with her, but it wasn't about them. It was about my mom and what it meant for *us*. She didn't say anything when she came back to the pew. She just sat down next to me and we continued to listen to the rest of the service. But the tension wasn't as heavy, and the air felt lighter. Suddenly it wasn't all about my mom, it was about *me*. It didn't matter that this was the first time she had stood up for me like that, something inside me felt changed. Even Alex joined in with the singing.

Alex went to bed early tonight, and I stayed on the porch with Mom. The best thing about Colorado this time of year is the smell of pine trees. You can smell pine trees for miles. The sun was setting, and the hum of birds were calling the night.

"I liked your speech, Mom."

She didn't say anything for a moment, but she was smiling. Then she said, "It's a start."

"I don't want to fight anymore." Today had been so good and I was afraid she was going to launch into one of her lectures.

"I mean a start for us. You have always been the most important thing in my life. It's my fault, Kayden, everything that has happened. The way I acted was my fault."

I wondered if she would choose to do it all over again if she could.

"I didn't understand," she said, "but I do now. I have spent time trying to understand you, Kayden."

"Why now?"

She sipped her tea, looked out at the mountains, and said that she had met a woman in the grocery store. The woman was new in town, so Mom invited her to the church. Over months she told Mom that she had moved with her husband to Edmonson because their old life was too painful to live in. More months went by and the woman told Mom that she'd had a daughter, and the daughter had taken her life last spring.

"She was gay."

I didn't say anything, just stared at my mug of coffee not knowing what to say.

"The woman comes to our church now; we have coffee together every Friday. We talk about her daughter and I talk about you. She's helping me to understand. I still have you. My friend doesn't have her daughter and Shaye's parents no longer have her, but I still have you. I want you to be happy and to always know love."

"I do know love. I've known what love feels like all this time, even before Shaye died. But this town responded with hate, they persecuted us for it."

I couldn't blame an entire town for Shaye's death, because I knew in the end it was sadness that took her away from the world.

"I can't speak for anyone else. I can only speak for myself."

"Like me," I said, "I spoke for myself and you thought I was punishing you."

Tears had welled in her eyes again, and I knew this conversation was hard for her.

"I was scared," she replied, "but I am not afraid anymore. I have prayed and I have cried and I have missed you so much. You are what is important to me, and I know that God loves you and I know that love is the answer. It has always been the answer."

It was with my best efforts that I didn't tell her that Alex doesn't believe in God. Maybe one day I will cross that bridge, but for now, I was happy sitting on the porch with her. There wasn't anger between us or long bouts of silence. There wasn't any blame or confusion. There was just this simple understanding. She finally understood that I am the way I am, and that it's not as a result of her.

Wherever I go in life, I hope I always choose love. I hope you do, too.

Thanks for listening,
Kayden

May 19, 2013

Dear Keeper,

Alex keeps asking when I will find out if I got into the marine program. I tell her I will soon, because I should know in a few days. But then she asks odd questions like if the people who run the program call the referrals I listed down on the application or if they know I work at the Marine

Center or if it's an anonymous ballot. It's definitely not an anonymous ballot, because I spent a whole week writing the application knowing that my name goes on the application form. I wanted everything to be as perfect as it could be. She has worked every day since the weekend we came back from visiting my mom in Colorado, but I have tried to see her as much as possible. I have also had exams, which I think I did fine on, but I don't want to jinx myself.

I enjoy the coffee at Green Leaf, especially when Alex makes it because she writes things on the paper cup if I have it to-go or draws hearts with chocolate dust in the milk for me. This morning she was super busy. There was at least double the amount of customer traffic. I usually sit at the counter because Alex is on the coffee machine and I can talk to her, but the counter was full today, so I slid into a table next to the brick wall. Green Leaf is rustic, with fairy lights hanging from the ceiling and paintings on the walls. Alex controls the speakers with her phone, so at least there's good music here. I counted each brick on the wall to the tune of Lily Allen who was faintly playing over the chatter, until I finally caught Alex's attention. I wanted to say hi, but I think she thought I meant 'bring me a coffee' because she placed a coffee cup on the table while moving around me and picking up a stack of empty mugs from another table and handing them to the other waitress.

I heard her say, "Pick up those feet, do I have to do everything for you?"

I could tell she was stressed.

Then I noticed the writing on the coffee cup:

It's so busy – you look pretty

I wrote back a message and asked the waitress to take it to her.

Then another coffee cup was placed on the table.

Finish at 4, exams all done?

I sent the waitress back.

Another one.

Proud of you

I was quite content having a conversation through paper coffee cups, but when I looked over at her, she was looking at her phone and seemed even more stressed out than what Green Leaf had made her.

I sent my coffee cup back asking if she was okay.

But the cup that came back said,

Brandon texted again

Suddenly I didn't feel like drawing on any more coffee cups. Brandon texts Alex more every day. I don't care that he texts her, I care that she texts him back. Also, I don't trust Brandon. He's smart and he does great work for the otters at the Marine Center, but he makes me feel weird. It's not the type of weird you get when the person you love's ex is always hanging around, either. It's a different kind of weird and I can't explain it. And the most confusing part is that Alex has been to lunch with him twice. Even after everything she told me about him, he's still somehow in her life. She tells me it's because I have to work with him and she doesn't want to make it awkward, but that doesn't make any sense to me. She changes the subject when she hears his name and she tenses when I try to ask her about why she's been texting him.

Dad brought tacos home for dinner and I asked him why some people still talk to the ones that hurt them so much.

He said, "Maybe they feel like that person has something over them."

"Like a secret?"

He nodded with a mouthful of food.

"So how do you get them to tell you the secret if the other person is making them keep it from you?"

"I'm nacho about that one, kiddo," and he grinned with bits of lettuce and ranch stuck in his teeth.

I said something like, "Taco Bell should definitely hire you, Dad," and decided I wasn't very hungry.

I have been so busy sharing that I forgot maybe other people don't share. But I thought my girlfriend *was* sharing with me. What if she has secrets, too, but the difference is that she doesn't share them with me anymore?

Things feel like they are crashing. Please don't let me become stuck again, I don't want to become stuck again.

Thanks for listening,
Kayden

May 22, 2013

Dear Keeper,

I just got home. I never thought I would ever live to graduate. This probably sounds a little intense, and I know it's been a while since I have had bad thoughts, but I am just proud, because I never thought I would get here. My school has white gowns, so when I came down the stairs dressed in my gown and cap, my dad announced that I looked like an angel. He was standing in the doorway with his phone trying to record everything. Alex had to help him because he's not so great with touch screens.

He said to Alex, "Get a full screen shot of her gown."

"Oh don't worry, Mr. S, I will."

When I reached her and tried to get her to stop filming, she whispered, "Hi, angel," and I told her to quit it.

I was nervous in the car. I was worried about going on stage to accept my diploma and tripping over something. Nate is also graduating and so are Tyler and Joe. Tyler might be going to Washington in the fall next year and Joe has an internship at Long Island Hospital for disease research. Nate has an interview with the reserves for the New York Lizards. When he told me last week, he had tears in his eyes because he never thought it would happen. I am so proud of my friends, and my therapist was right: you want to be around to see things like this. After speeches and awards, they played Macklemore as we threw our caps up into the air, and there was lots of cheering and some girls were crying. The word of the afternoon was congratulations. It came out of nearly every person's mouth at least three times. After the crowd had dispersed and people were talking with their families, Professor Martin came up to my dad and shook his hand.

"Kayden is very intelligent and has a great passion for marine animals."

"Thank you," my dad said, and his chest was puffed out and his cheeks were that rosy kind of pink when you are very happy about something.

Then she shook my hand. "It's been a pleasure, Kayden."

"Thanks for everything, Professor."

"I think you should be proud of how far you've come."

She gave me that look to say she knew I had secrets, but it was okay because I knew she had secrets, too.

I also found out that I was accepted into the marine program. They said if I do well in the program, they will give me a credit reference to work with manta rays in Hawaii. Can you believe that? I told Kip, and he said that Mahala would be very happy about this. I liked that he said that. Then Nate said there was a party at his house, which I knew there was going to be anyway. It was a good party because Joe and Nate are friends again and Joe doesn't seem so sad anymore. We drank champagne because Tyler said it was custom at graduations. I think he made that up, but champagne is custom at celebrations, and I supposed we were all celebrating. And I danced with Alex. Her hair is lighter and there aren't colors streaked through it anymore. She looks older and wiser and more serious, but she still laughs when I try to be funny. I am in love with her laugh. There was loud music and soft music and beer pong and I think one of Nate's lacrosse friends streaked on a dare. Everybody always says things change when you graduate high school and then again when you graduate college. My therapist spent years explaining that change isn't necessarily a bad thing, but I hoped that all of this wouldn't change. I still wanted Nate to be my best friend. I still wanted to go to Shakedown's with Tyler and Joe. I still wanted to be in love with Alex. I always want to be in love with Alex. But she seems far away lately, like she is thinking of something else.

And then when she comes back to me, she is as she always is: funny and generous and confident and smart. I just want her to stay.

Thanks for listening,
Kayden

summer

the rest

June 22, 2013

Dear Keeper,

Just so you know, I have been meaning to write. I truly have, but things have been sort of like a roller coaster. I have been busy "sharing" which as it turns out, Alex has not been busy doing. After graduation, I tried to talk to her more about moving to California. I told her that she didn't have to come right away, that she could come whenever she wanted. Every time I brought up California, she changed the subject. Then I was busy packing and working at the Marine Center. And I was busy trying to spend time with Nate and my dad. And then I started to share things with them, too, like how hard it all was, but how I am better now. I think my dad liked that I shared that with him. I think it made him feel better about me moving across the country. Then I had to do more shopping and packing. I felt the anxiety creeping up on me, but then Nate would come over in the nights and we'd watch old movies and I would be okay again. Sometimes Joe and Tyler would come over and they would smoke and it would calm me down even though I wasn't doing it with them. It's not like I am not ready to go to California, I'm just not ready to go without Alex.

Yesterday was my last shift at the Marine Center. I feel excited to be able to do something that feels greater than myself, but I also feel sad because I love this place. I went to every exhibit today and I said goodbye to every animal. And then I sat in Ray Bay. I watched people come and go and stare at the display like it was the most beautiful thing they had ever seen. And then Kip found me and he gave me a stuffed manta ray from the gift shop.

"You know something, Rayden? I am going to miss you around here."

"Kip, please don't make me cry."

He pretended to be bewildered, "You cry?"

"Not so much anymore."

He sat down next to me on the bench.

"You've come a hell of a way, kid."

"Didn't think I would, did you?"

"You're wrong about that. Always knew you had it in you."

"Thanks for always looking out for me."

He grinned. "You bet. Thanks for being another daughter."

When he said that, I did cry. Because I love Kip and I love the marina and I love the Marine Center and part of me didn't want to leave. Part of me wanted to stay in Long Island, to keep it forever.

"Do you think Long Island is going to keep all my secrets safe?"

He thought on this for a moment. "Yes I do," he said finally, "I think you'll always have a home here, no matter what other places you share yourself with."

And then I hugged him, because work policy doesn't apply to Kip anymore, and he's not just a colleague, he's my friend.

Then I texted Alex and told her to meet me at the marina. It's summer and it's hot, so I thought we could have a picnic by the water and just talk about things. Things were okay at first. She asked me how my last day was and she made a comment about seeing my dad to service her car. And then I asked her again.

"Come with me."

Every time I ask, she looks at me like I have given her the best and the worst news in the world.

Then I said, "I want you to come with me. We can do anything together, Alex. I love you and I want to be with you wherever I go."

She said, "I can't just pick up and leave my life, Kayden. I have a job and my family is here."

"But I don't understand. In Colorado, you said you would go anywhere with someone who understands you."

"Well things change. I can't just leave my family. They need me."

"Can you leave me?" I asked.

"That's not fair," and she looked away. "You can't ask me to leave everything behind for you."

I can't get that last thing she said out of my head.

I leave tomorrow. I have packed up my things and Nate is watching It's a Wonderful Life with me on the couch.

"Do you think she'll come with me?"

"She's probably just scared, Peanut. Try not to worry."

"I guess."

"Besides, it's our last night watching old movies together."

"Can't you move to California, too?"

He laughed and stuck his hand in the popcorn, "Any lacrosse teams for me to join?"

"What about baseball instead?"

"Or surfing?"

I cracked up thinking about Nate trying to surf, and he threw a handful of popcorn at me.

"California is going to be great, Peanut, you'll see."

Alex still hasn't told me if she's coming or not, but I bought her a ticket anyway. You probably think that's a crazy thing to do, but if you love someone you just want them to love you back. Alex said she would follow me anywhere.

I know she loves me.

I know it.

Thanks for listening,
Kayden

June 23, 2013

Dear Keeper,

Alex didn't come with me.

I waited in the departure lounge until the last call for the flight. Until all the passengers had emptied, and it was just me. Holding my ticket and the ticket for the girl I loved. Only it seems that she doesn't love me back anymore. My eyes stung as I handed my ticket to be scanned, they watered as I walked down the terminal and boarded the aircraft, and they were red by the time the plane lifted into the air. It was dark outside, and I wondered how many times my heart was going to die before I landed in California.

On the plane, I thought about how she hadn't been there. I went to the bathroom three times because I thought

I was going to have a panic attack and didn't want to do it in front of the whole plane. I don't understand anything; I am so confused. I wish I wasn't in love with Alex. I wish we had just stayed friends. Maybe then I wouldn't be in so much pain.

Thanks for listening,
Kayden

June 26, 2013

Dear Keeper,

So, I did fall. But I got back up again. I fell, I got back up, I fell, I got back up. I think that's what life is. Things happen, but that doesn't mean it's all over. Also, when your heart breaks, don't listen to Adele or Boyz II Men. I mean, you can. But you will cry. Adele says we could have had it all. I thought Alex and I had it all, but now it seems like we don't. Boyz II Men sing about the end of the road. I thought my road with Alex would be forever. I don't think I can walk on a road without her. So far, I have cried myself to sleep ever since I got to California and I'm sure my roommate must think I am an emotional basket case. Why is it that every time I am the new person in town, people think I'm a mess? On second thought, don't answer that.

Alex and I were perfect a month ago. How do things change so quickly? One minute we were in love and the next she didn't want to be with me. It doesn't make any sense. I bought a car a few days ago. It's nothing like my old truck. I miss that truck. This one is a beat-up station wagon that looks like it's been owned by five different surfers. There's a dent in the back and the panel on the right side of the car is painted blue. My dad would have a heart attack if he saw the condition it was in, but at least it turns on and the engine doesn't sound clunky. I start the marine program in a couple of days. I am living in a town called Olsen Bay, and I wanted to get settled first, unpack my things, figure out where the closest pizza shop is and how far it is to the beach. I discovered that the pizza shop is a ten-minute walk from my apartment building, the beach is fifteen, and the marine hospital is a twenty-minute drive. Last night I thought about leaving it all behind and going back to Long Island. I got all the way to the parking garage underneath my building and I sat inside my car. The car seats are frayed and the radio doesn't work. My radio doesn't even work out here because the only frequency that works is from that radio station in Long Island.

I think I must have sat there in silence until three in the morning. It doesn't even feel like my heart is in my body. It feels like it's somewhere else and I am trying to find it, but I can't because Alex has hidden it from me. You can't predict other people, not even when you think you know them. I have tried so hard to understand why she suddenly changed her mind, but it only makes the thoughts loud again. But we didn't *actually* break up. It's not like a ceramic mug that is knocked from a ledge and you see all the pieces shatter.

I got on a plane and Alex didn't follow me.
Where do you go from there?

Thanks for listening,
Kayden

June 28, 2013

Dear Keeper,

I just got home because I was stuck in traffic. The traffic out here is busier than East Point, especially on Friday afternoons. Also, the people in Olsen Bay aren't like people in East Point, but I strangely like it. I started the marine program today. I am one of three other interns. There is Lewis, he's from New Jersey, and Kelly and Emma who are both from San Diego. Lewis also likes manta rays, so we have lots to talk about. Part of the reason why I applied was because I wanted to be part of their first response team. We go in groups of six to rescue injured marine life and bring them back to the marine hospital. Sort of like a paramedic, only for sea turtles and otters and other marine life living along the coastline. There is also a division that specializes in manta ray research, which made my heart race. The first day of any program is usually quite simple. It was the same type of introduction seminar I had when I first started at the Marine Center, although the manual is bigger than all of my textbooks in college combined. On the front, it says "Rescue, Rehabilitate & Release" in big bold letters. I think I am going to enjoy being in this program. My window looks out onto the street and I can hear someone blasting Bruno Mars. I wish they wouldn't because it makes me think of Alex and Nate's parties and dancing until we couldn't stop laughing. I live on a quiet street on an apartment block that has a giant lemon tree out front. Yesterday I called Kip and told him about the program and my first day. Then I asked if he had seen Alex around and he said he hadn't. He said he had been avoiding Brandon as well. Then he told me he was sure things would work out with Alex, and he was certain that something else was going on that she hadn't told me about. But I said Alex always tells me everything, so I don't know what to believe. I miss my dad and Mr. Koi's. I miss watching old movies with Nate because they always filled a space that opens up when I am sad. But I need to keep going because it's what Mahala would want me to do.

Also, my hair is always salty because I can't keep away from the beach. I used to swim a lot back in Long Island at the rockpools, but it's not the same. The beach here stretches for miles, the sun stays out later, and the air is much warmer. I think about Mahala when I am in the ocean. I like to imagine her soul is out there somewhere; I can hear it every time a wave passes over me. The sand feels different here, too. It's crisp, like the sun takes pride in baking it for so long. I think I might go for a run before dinner tonight. I have a choice between a bowl of noodles or a bowl of noodles. Also, during my lunch break I got a text from Alex. She told me that she was back together with Brandon and that she couldn't come see me. She said this because last night I texted her and asked her to come to California. The message said "read" almost immediately but then she didn't reply until today. Then I had to finish the rest of my day with my heart in my throat. I think I went on auto pilot after she texted. I suppose this helped, because that traffic I just sat in was not fun. I might even still be on auto pilot because I don't even care about the fact that I only have noodles to eat tonight. Maybe I will just sleep on the beach. I need to stay calm because I have a job interview tomorrow. I just hope when they ask me why I want the job, I don't say, "So I won't think about Alex every second of the day."

Thanks for listening,
Kayden

June 29, 2013

Dear Keeper,

My roommate's name is Amelia. She knew John from college, and back in East Point he told me she was looking for someone to move in. She's in her late twenties and loves dogs. Even her toaster is in the shape of a dog. The apartment almost always smells like incense and the fridge is always filled with watermelon. I want to ask her if she is gay because I think she is, but I don't want to make things weird if she isn't. I know she is an activist against dog fighting because there are always new flyers on the kitchen counter advertising new protests. I have been meaning to ask her if I can come to one, but I have also been heartbroken. When you are heartbroken you can't seem to do anything unless you absolutely have to. Her friend Elliot is staying on the couch because his apartment is being repainted. He says he is allergic to the smell of paint but Amelia says he's just using it as an excuse because his ex-girlfriend is moving out and he doesn't want to be there. Avoiding paint or ex-girlfriends are both reasonable excuses in my opinion. Just so you know, Elliot used to be called Elle. On my second night in the apartment, I couldn't stop thinking about kissing Alex so I decided to buy two bottles of wine and drink them both. I sat on the balcony and listened to the distant waves for what felt like hours until Elliot asked if he could sit with me. He also brought more wine. After our third bottle, he told me that he had finished his medical transition about a year ago, but there was still a long way to go. I said, "I like Elliot more," and he didn't stop smiling for the rest of the night. But truly, I think Elliot suits him more, and this is probably because this is who he was always meant to be.

Elliot works at a bar in town. It's called Beckett's Bar, and he's the chef there. This is also the place I had my interview yesterday. Elliot lined it up when I told him I didn't have a job and the search hadn't been going very well. Before the interview, Amelia lent me some nicer clothes to wear. I've only ever worn the Marine Center uniform, and other than t-shirts and jeans, my wardrobe selection isn't that big. Elliot told me to just be myself but I was still nervous. I'd never had a proper interview before; I wasn't sure what to say or do with my hands. The bar manager's name is Sarah. She was wearing a denim vest and told me she was "hungover as shit" as soon as I sat down. The other person, Jason, is the restaurant manager, and he said "I'll be hungover tomorrow." Then they asked me a few questions like where I was from and to list how many types of beers I knew. I listed twenty brands and told them about Kip's cocktail recipe book that I read cover to cover. Then Sarah told me I was hired. I didn't think I heard her right, so I said, "Really?" and Jason asked if I could start tomorrow. I said yes and now I have a job. I called Elliot and he was super excited about this. He told me to come home immediately because we were going out to celebrate. I've never had anyone celebrate me getting a job before, so I said I would.

By the time I got back to the apartment, they were dressed and ready to go. I hadn't finished laundry, so Elliot told me I could wear his clothes. His jeans were too big so the rips showed half my legs and Amelia told me I should wear them more often. Then this girl showed up to the apartment and she had big bouncy curls and was wearing a dress with cat paw prints all over it and she kissed Amelia. This confirmed a number of things about why John had suggested I rent this apartment. We went to a bar near the beach. It looked like it had been a crab shack and they just added a bar and some live music. Elliot said it was one of the best bars in town, besides Beckett's Bar. There were people making out everywhere, other people were fighting, most people were drinking, things like that.

At one point in the night, I thought I saw Alex in the

crowd, but when I reached her, the girl's face wasn't Alex's. I wanted to go home and cry on Nate's shoulder, but I am meant to be brave and handling things out here.

Thanks for listening,
Kayden

July 1, 2013

Dear Keeper,

Sometimes heartbreak isn't about how long it takes you to fall asleep because you can't stop thinking about the day you both said I love you. Sometimes it's not even about staying busy and surrounding yourself with the things that make you happy because you still feel sad. Sometimes heartbreak is as simple as staring at the shelf of chocolate in the grocery store aisle and not knowing which one to choose because you used to always get her favorite. It's only Monday but I'm so tired from everything we are doing and learning in the marine program. I called my dad when I got home because he wanted an update on how everything was going. It's not where I am that needs updating, everything is good here. I like my roommate and I like her friends. I like the leaders of the marine program and my colleagues. It's Long Island that my thoughts keep coming back to. Long Island is where Alex is.

Dad picked up on the first ring and said "Hey, kid."

"Hi, Dad."

"How was your day?"

"It was fine. Lifeguards called in a sea lion on the beach, so we went down there and he was injured. We got him back to the hospital though, so he should be okay."

"That sounds intense, kid."

"Yeah. But I love it out here, Dad."

This is the truth. My apartment isn't far from the beach, and I like sitting out on the balcony in the late afternoons. You can see big palm trees in the distance and poppies along the streets. Olsen Bay smells like salt and sand and a little bit of honey.

"Have you spoken to Alex?"

My heart turned over at the sound of her name. It was so strange to hear my dad ask about her so casually.

I said, "No," and then I told him that some nights I could feel the cracks in my heart. But at the same time, I felt different.

He paused for a second and then asked, "What do you mean 'different'?"

"I mean I'm not afraid that the cracks are there, because I know it'll get better."

My dad doesn't really give long speeches or anything like that. He doesn't even usually say anything profound, so when he said, "Well when there's cracks, it means the light can shine through," I was taken aback.

"Dad, have you been reading poetry books?"

He laughed and it crackled through the phone line, "Just let the light in, kid. It's good for you."

I told him I would and I told him I would call again at the end of the week. After I hung up, I went to the kitchen to make food. I made grilled cheese because pay day isn't until Wednesday this week. I'd had two mouthfuls and Elliot came through the front door with food. It smelled like Mr. Koi's from East Point and made me miss nights with Nate and fried rice and dumplings. Elliot told me that my grilled cheese looked burned and he made a plate for me. Then he asked if I wanted to watch Seinfield reruns, so we watched twenty-six episodes in a row. I think Elliot understands sadness in the same way I do. Alex once told me that you should tell people they are worth something while they're alive, not write it on their Facebook page or in cards with flowers after they've gone.

"Elliot," I said, before he put the next episode on, "you're worth something."

He grinned and asked if I was high. I said no, I just felt like saying it.

"You're worth something, too."

I wish Alex were here; I think she'd like Elliot.

Thanks for listening,
Kayden

July 4, 2013

Dear Keeper,

I don't know if I will ever see Alex again, but her name echoes in my mind when I am trying to sleep. I think about all those nights I would move in my bed and feel her pressed against me. You just don't get over something like that, at least not entirely. You share everything with someone and then suddenly they're gone. I still love Alex. I love her so much and I didn't know that the ache could be so heavy I feel it in my bones. I don't understand why she would go back to Brandon. He couldn't possibly love her in the same way I do. I love Alex more than I love the entire ocean, and I thought she loved me back.

Everybody is celebrating today, but I don't feel like being very festive. Amelia had a party tonight and she invited some of her friends. I can't remember anyone's names, but I didn't really want to talk to them anyway. After they had been drinking enough that they wouldn't notice if I slipped away, I took a bottle of wine and went to my room. When I first moved into this apartment, I tried to make it look like home. I put up old movie posters on the wall, *The Wizard of Oz* hangs above my bed, there's picture frames of Nate, Tyler, and Joe and also of my dad and Kip. There is the one of Mahala and I on my bedside. Elliot was really drunk a few nights back and he stole a traffic cone and left it in my room. It's next to my desk. There is a picture of Alex and I on my desk too, because I can't bring myself to throw it away. She wasn't just my morning and my late night, she was whole damn day. She listened to all my secrets, she told me that it was okay to be sad and hurt and scared. She reminded me that I can be all those things and still live.

My laundry basket is full, but I don't have enough quarters for the machine downstairs. I just wanted to drink myself to sleep. Then I heard knocking at my door. It was so soft at first I didn't think someone was actually knocking, but then the knocking turned into a pattern or a song that I couldn't remember.

"Kayden!"

I opened my door and let Elliot inside.

"Why are you here alone and not at the party?"

"The party is in the living room, I'm not that far away."

"I know but I missed you."

He reminded me of Nate in so many ways.

Then he saw the wine bottle and the glass. "I thought you didn't drink that much."

"I changed my mind."

He thought a moment and then he slid down onto my floor against the wall.

"But why are you drinking?"

"Because I love a girl and she loves someone else."

"How do you know she loves this someone else?"

"She told me."

He reached and tapped his champagne glass against mine, "This calls for vodka, not wine."

Then I asked, "Why are you drinking?"

"I'm sad."

"I'm sad, too. I was sad for such a long time and then a girl reminded me of who I was when I was happy. And it felt good." I stopped because I was going to cry again. I still feel like crying, which makes me angry because I just want to finish writing this all down for you.

"What did she do with your happiness?"

"Dropped it and didn't tell me why."

"They do that."

"Why?"

Then he shrugged and said people are selfish. "My last relationship was a mess. She was with me before my transition. We did all this talking all the time and soon that talking turned into arguing a lot. She wanted to be in an open relationship and I just wanted her. In the end after she'd spent all my money, she left California with some other dude."

I said "Fuck," in response, because what other word is there for something like that?

"I've never met someone more selfish than my ex, Kayden."

I couldn't tell if his eyes were watery from the alcohol or if he had started to cry.

"You deserve more."

"You too."

But I didn't know whether I did. How do you really know how you deserved to be loved? It's not like we come with an instruction manual: "Please handle with care or rock her world." It's not like you can open the book and it's going to read: "Has been hurt before, don't be too reckless with her heart." Because even when you tell people that and they know, they still do it anyway.

He stood up. "I'm getting the vodka."

"Elliot?"

"Yeah?"

"It's okay to be sad."

He smiled and said he knew and that tomorrow would still come.

Now he's asleep on my beanbag. He's snoring softly but

that might just be because we drank a lot. It's not even midnight and I can still hear people in the living room. They're laughing about something on the TV. You probably think I've become stuck again, but I haven't. It's a strange feeling. I feel like my heart has been ripped into a thousand tiny pieces, but I'm still here and I know that I'll get back up again.

Happy Fourth.

Thanks for listening,
Kayden

July 15, 2013

Dear Keeper,

So I have news. I am confused by it, but I need to share it with you anyway. Before I get to that, I just wanted to say that I really like working at Beckett's Bar. Elliot cooks the best cheeseburger you will ever have in your life (which is saying something because I thought East Point had the best burgers), and sometimes we stay late after our shift and have beers because our boss is pretty cool. Sarah and Jason are actually more put together than I first thought. Sarah likes my taste in music. I got her a Sleepy Ears CD and she's been playing it at work. I also like the other waitstaff I work with, especially Grace. She really helped me out in the first few shifts while I tried to memorize the floor plan and the menu. Plus her kids love aquariums, so she likes to help me when I have task research for the marine program. Last night, a table of nine walked in late so we had to stay open longer than usual. Once the orders had piled up on the table, I went out back with Grace while she had a smoke.

"You smoke?"

"No."

"Good girl."

She reminds me of Kip and it makes me miss him more than I already do.

"They'll kill me, these things, lord knows I need to give it up?"

I said something like, "Anything can kill us," which probably sounded really morbid, but Grace didn't seem to mind. And even if she did, she didn't say anything.

"You missing your folks?"

"I miss my dad."

She inhaled and exhaled. The puffs of smoke hovered between us in the same way the truth does when it doesn't have anywhere else to go.

"And Kip and Nate, and…" I trailed off.

"What about the girl?"

There are moments in your life where you think people kind of know you, but it turns out they really know you.

"What girl?"

"Alex."

"How do you know about Alex?"

"Well you told me a little at the staff party."

Beckett's Bar had a staff party to celebrate ten years of

243

being open and it was only my fourth shift but I went anyway and I got really drunk and maybe I said some stuff to Grace, but I can't remember if I said Alex's name because I have been trying really hard not to say it.

I must have looked confused or sad or even both because then Grace said, "She came in looking for you the other day."

It's easy for me to tell you how I felt in that moment because the feeling hasn't gone away since. I was up all night with the feeling and all day at the marine hospital and even now it still sits in the pit of my stomach. I feel the way you do when you are excited by something but it lets you down and you don't know how something that could hurt you still makes your heart race as if it had never hurt you in the first place.

Alex excited me from the day I found her first letter. Since that day, she has excited me in more ways than I ever knew existed, until that day in June when she let me down. It is not a crumbling sadness that I feel when I think about her. It's not the kind of sadness that makes me want to bury myself. It's the kind of sadness that lingers after her name is spoken because I miss the way she says my name. And then afterward I am okay again, a little stronger. I told Grace that I needed one of her cigarettes and she lit one for me and we stood out there for a long time.

"Did she say anything else?"

"Just asked when your next shift was."

"What did you say?"

Grace lit up another cigarette, too.

"Asked her if she was the ex, and she nodded. Then I said she can come looking for you, but I'm not about to tell her anything, not at my place."

"She said she was my ex?"

Grace looked at me, "That's all you got from that, not the fact that she's here? Didn't you say you was from Long Island, child? That's an awful long way."

I couldn't believe Alex was in California, I was having trouble processing it all. "I can't believe she's here. Why now?" I was mostly asking this to myself, but Grace told me what she thought anyway.

"Hon, someone doesn't cross the country if they don't have something to say."

"She hurt me."

Grace inhaled, thought a while, nodded and exhaled.

"We all hurt each other sometimes"

I dragged in, felt the smoke fill my lungs, breathed out, felt the dizziness catch me.

"I guess."

"You want me to tell you when she shows up next?"

"Yes."

"No problem."

"Did she say how she found out where I was working?"

"Not a clue, love."

"Probably my dad."

"Mmm?"

"Nothing, we better get back to work."

"You need a minute, love?"

"No, I'm okay."

"You sure? Why don't you go dust down the bar, love? I'll clear their plates."

"It's okay, I can manage. I'm gonna help you."

She laughed, a raspy kind of laugh that reminded me of all the times Kip would let out his howl in the Marine Center because a crab had latched onto my finger and wouldn't let go.

"You just get right back up on your horse, don't you? You'll be fine, hon."

The light from the kitchen was shining over her face, and even though Grace was older than my mom, I still thought she was beautiful. It made me think that maybe being beautiful is more about how you treat someone when they are sad rather than how you look.

This is when things got strange, because Nate called me at 2am this morning. He sounded angry, but he also sounded drunk.

"What's wrong?"

"I'm going to kill Brandon."

"What?"

"I'm going to kill that fucker, Peanut, rip his lowlife head off."

"Nate! What is going on?"

"Is Alex with you?"

"Why the hell would Alex be with me?"

"There was a massive blowout at Green Leaf plates flying everywhere. Alex quit. She got on a plane, too, she's coming for you."

"Nate!"

There was noise in the background and Joe was yelling at Nate to stop acting like an idiot.

"Put Joe on the phone!"

More noise, crashes of broken bottles.

"Kayden?"

"Joe? What's going on?"

"It's okay, Nate is just drunk. I'm sober, I'll get him home."

"Why was he talking about Brandon? Where's Alex?"

"Just talk to her, Kayden, you have to hear her out. All this shit is messed up, but it wasn't her fault."

"Joe, talk to me, I need you to just—"

"Nate, get off the fucking fence. Kayden? I love you, I'm sorry, talk to Alex."

Then the call disconnected.

When I woke up this morning Nate had texted me.

I'm sorry, Peanut. Just talk to Alex. Love you.

Everyone knew that Alex had flown to California but me, and no one had told me. I don't understand what is going on.

Thanks for listening,
Kayden

July 18, 2013

Dear Keeper,

I know it's stupid, but I have been looking for Alex. Every shift, I stare out the window hoping she will walk past. I wonder if she's in Olsen Bay and how long she is going to be here and if she really is looking for me. So today at work when I was sitting down in one of the booths during my break reading one of the many manuals for the marine program, and the wind was coming in through the window, and I was thinking about the way Alex smells and her laugh, I wasn't expecting her to suddenly slide into the booth in front of me and place a coffee cup in between us. The first thing I saw was not her, but I didn't need to, because I know the shape of her face and her body and the tone of her skin. The first thing I saw was the coffee cup and the words, "I'm sorry," written on it.

I have thought about her ever since I left Long Island. I have wondered what I would do if I could just talk to her in person. So even I was surprised when I moved the coffee cup to the end of the table and went back to reading my textbook.

She moved, drew a pen from her pocket, wrote on the cup again, placed it in front of me.

Please can we talk?

I took the pen from her and wrote,

You hurt me

I caught her reaction as she wrote back, and she looked like she was about to start crying. She'd better not, because

I hate it when Alex cries.

She wrote,

I know, but I love you, please

I said aloud, "You can't just come here and write on coffee cups and expect me to just write back 'All good.'"

"I know that."

"What are you doing here?"

"I need to talk to you."

"Well you've got fifteen minutes because that's when my break ends."

She took a deep breath and said, "I've been selfish and I've lied to you."

"You left me standing in an airport all by myself."

"Kayden, I never said I was coming with you, I didn't want you to buy that ticket!"

"Of course I was going to buy it Alex, I'm fucking in love with you."

"And I'm in love with you!"

This was an awfully weird way to show someone that you love them. I don't even think my therapist would have an explanation for this.

"The truth is Brandon screwed me again."

"You slept with him?"

"No! Kayden that's not..." She brushed her hands through her hair. "I mean he fucked me over. The only reason I was texting him, seeing him, was because..."

She was silent again.

"If you came all the way to California just to make up some story, Alex, I don't want to hear it."

"He told me that he would make sure you didn't get in."

"Get in where?"

"To the program. He said he would call the people he knew at the administration and have you eliminated from any chance of getting in."

"What?"

"He said he would do that if I didn't go back to him. The whole reason he transferred back to East Point was to get me back. When he found out about us, he put two and two together and assumed I would go to California with you. So he decided to blackmail me."

"Alex, I—"

"I had to look at you and look at your face every time you asked me to come with you and I had to pretend that I didn't want to come. I had to tell you that I didn't love you, when none of that is true."

I felt sick and I needed to know. "Did he touch you?"

"No. I didn't let it get that far. He came to Green Leaf and told me that I had to move in with him and I lost it. I called the marine program and I asked if anyone knew who he was and they said no. So I told Nate and Joe and they went crazy. Then Brandon came to my house and my mom called the cops and I just fucking left and got on a plane."

The amount of hatred I felt towards Brandon in that moment was enough to bleed out of my ears.

"And I've been texting Kip the whole time and he pulled some strings to get me to talk with your boss."

"You spoke with my boss?" When did any of this happen, how did I not know about any of this?

She nodded. "Yes, and he confirmed that none of them have any idea who Brandon is."

"Fuck." Because as I have said before, what else can you say in a situation like this? Then I said, "Is this what Nate meant when he said he was going to kill Brandon?"

"How do you know about that?"

"He called me."

Alex sighed and ran her hands through her hair again. Her hair was shorter, darker than before.

"I was cleaning my room and I found those photos of us, the ones at the Butterfly House, and we took those pictures in the photo booth and I just," she paused, her lips trembling, "I just got so sad and so angry and scared and so I called Nate and I asked him to help me because I didn't know what to do."

"So you never got back together with him?"

"Of course not, Kayden, I was trying to figure out a way to get away from Brandon without him ruining your dreams."

"You should have told me about Brandon. We would have figured something out. I don't want you to ever be unhappy to make me happy. That's not the way that we should be."

Alex looked so sad. She took a marker from her bag and began to write letters on the coffee cup. It took me a moment to realize she was spelling out, "I'm so sorry." Then she pushed the coffee cup in front of me and wrote it again and again until it filled up the rest of the space.

I do love her. I loved her a year ago, I loved her three months ago, I love her now.

"I have a friend," I said, "and she was lost and scared of her own sadness. Then a girl came into her life and believed in her so much that slowly she started to believe in herself, too."

Alex had started to cry.

"But then the girl got caught up and suddenly everything seemed to crash and burn in her path, so she needed to figure it all out."

"And did the friend understand in the end? Did she figure it out?"

"She figured something else out."

She whispered, "What?"

"She couldn't burn the somebody who could hold fire."

Alex said, "Kayden," in the way she has always said my name, and I closed the space between us over the table. We kissed. We kissed harder than we have ever kissed, and it did burn. It burned right down to the tips of my toes. But it didn't hurt. It brought me back to life.

Kip was right. The ocean always returns.

Thanks for listening,
Kayden

July 24, 2013

Dear Keeper,

I finally understand the damage that is caused when you don't share things. Alex didn't share with me what was going on and it almost ruined us. We have talked more about what happened, and I understand why she chose not to tell me, but she also promised she wouldn't keep anything from me again. Alex has stayed the whole week. When she saw the car I was now driving, she stood out in the street laughing for fifteen minutes. I wanted to take her out for ice cream, but I made her pay after her relentless teasing. California is hot and humid and my air conditioner is busted. Alex had the window down with her hand stretched out making waves in the air.

"I got you something," she said.

"What?"

She reached into her bag and pulled out a small hand held radio.

"This one has Californian frequency."

I tried hard to concentrate on the road and not lean over to kiss her. Alex switched it on and The Temptations were playing. The song was *My Girl* and I remembered my accident.

"This song was on when I was driving to you that night."

"The night of your accident?"

I nodded.

"I'm glad you're my girl, you know that right?"

I reached for her hand and pressed it to my lips, "I know."

"Even though you drive a total shit box."

She squealed as I bit into her knuckles.

The air and salt here gets in your hair and sticks to your skin and you feel like you are walking around breathing in the sea. I love working in the marine program, and I love living here. But I want Alex to live here, too.

After the program today, I wanted to take her to the

beach. I packed up a bag and a rug and we walked down and found a spot just near the wharf.

She said it was just like sitting on the marina.

"But bigger," I added.

She laughed, and it was that familiar laugh, like I had her back again.

Then I asked, "Do you think about all the memories we've made?"

"I think about you all the time, does that count?"

"No I just mean everything that's happened, those are memories I have, but also memories you have."

She dug her toes into the sand but didn't take her eyes off me. Those same eyes with that same intensity and that same color changing with the time of day.

"I want to always make memories with you, Kayden."

"I wish you could stay. I don't want you to go back to Long Island."

She moved so she could sit between my legs and lean back into my chest.

"Well I have to pack and get my stuff."

Either I had been distracted and imagined seeing Mahala in between the waves or I hadn't heard Alex properly.

"You have to what?"

"Pack."

"Pack what?"

Alex laughed, "My stuff, you idiot."

"You mean?"

She nodded, "Nate is going to come visit, we're going to drive my car down here."

"You'll never make it."

She laughed again, "That's what Kip said until I had your dad service it. Should be all good to go. Fill my car up and drive out to meet this girl."

"Do I know this girl?"

She kissed me, slowly. "She's a friend of yours."

"Lucky friend."

Alex whispered, "I think so, too," before we fell back onto the rug. I'm too giddy to write anything else.

Thanks for listening,
Kayden

August 5, 2013

Dear Keeper,

Things have been so busy and I have been sharing so much that the thoughts have quieted. I know I am always going to have thoughts, but if I keep sharing them, I don't think I will become stuck again. After Alex came out here and told me the truth about Brandon, things have changed between us. We are stronger than we were before. Like losing each other somehow made us closer. It was never going to be all about fireworks or roses. It never is.

My dad is going to visit me for Christmas this year. I'm excited but I will have to park my car around the block. Mom might even fly out here for Thanksgiving. I know that I will never have them over together, but I don't feel like I am the reason they fell apart anymore. I don't feel like I have to carry other people's pain, just my own, and that's enough. I still have my old movie posters on my wall but there are some significant changes. That half of the room also now belongs to Alex. We share it together. It's our room, our desk, our bed. The apartment feels like home, our home. Elliot moved back into his old apartment a couple weeks ago, but he still comes over for wine after work. He and Alex are great friends, just like I knew they would be. Alex started her own business. She called it "Mahala". She makes jewelry. I especially like her necklaces with the silver manta ray pendants. I have a few, octopus, manta ray, turtle, but that's because she's my girlfriend. And I've been meaning to tell you that we went to one of Amelia's protests. She's a very good speaker. She had a megaphone and everything, but that's another story to share.

The sadness doesn't come in waves like it used to. It still comes every now and then because things happen in life that make me sad. But it's the kind of sadness that sits on your front porch and asks you to share a moment of your time. The sadness isn't shadowing me anymore. It's a friend that, every now and then, needs me in its corner. Alex and I went to the beach with some beers and we sat and drank them as the tide went out and the sun faded away. I like to think the sadness went out with the tide, and even though the tide comes back again, it doesn't stay.

Thanks for listening,
Kayden

August 30, 2013

Dear Keeper,

It's been a long few weeks. We rescued a sea turtle in the harbor the other day. I am still trying to channel the adrenaline, because in the first response team, it's our job to save the animal and bring it safely back to the marine hospital. I wanted to write and say happy anniversary. I think we can have an anniversary because you have helped me so much. It's been 365 days since I told you my first secret. That's a long time for a secret keeper. The marine program is sending us to Hawaii next month for manta ray conservation week. That means I get to live and breathe manta rays for a whole week in Hawaii. I have also been thinking about what to do when these pages run out. There are not many left now. Alex says I should put you back in Long Island. She says it would be nice to keep you there. Nate has a game coming up next month and we are going back to support him. His first professional game! I am strangely excited to go back to East Point. Kip fired Brandon so he isn't in town anymore, but Kip has a new "lady friend" as he says. He said she can beat anyone in karaoke and she loves Shakedown's. I can't wait to meet her. I was thinking of making a home for you in my old campus library. Somewhere in between the marine science and chemistry textbooks. After all, that's where Alex and I first met. It feels like a good way to finish the last page. Besides, maybe you will help someone else like me. Maybe together we can remind a sad person that they are never alone.

Anyway, I'll think about it.

Thanks for listening,
Kayden

September 20, 2013

Dear Keeper,

I don't want to say goodbye after all this time. I've shared so much of myself with you, that it's hard to let go. You will always be someone in this world holding my secrets. I decided to leave you in the library after all. I hope you don't think this means I'm choosing to never write to you again – it's just I don't have any new secrets, at least ones that I don't already share with Alex. It's not like I'm choosing her over you or anything like that, it's just nice that she listens to me. It makes me feel like I am loved. It makes me feel safe, it gives me a purpose to stay and share my life because someone else is counting on me. I think that's cool.

But enough about me, you've listened to me for so long, I just want to make the last entry about you. I want to thank you for never asking me questions I didn't want to answer. I want to thank you for listening to me and not pressuring me to share when I wasn't ready. My heart was heavy when I first started writing to you, but now it feels lighter. So I want to thank you for existing, because I'm so grateful someone like you is alive in this world and able to listen to someone who was as sad as me. I hope you know that you are loved, and wherever you go in life, in the moments that you feel sad, I hope you remember how important you are to me and how much you helped me. And if you're sad and you're reading this, I hope you know that the sadness doesn't make you any less of a person. Just remember that one day it won't hurt so bad, and knowing you survived makes you believe you can do anything. And I think that's something worth keeping.

Thanks for listening,
Kayden

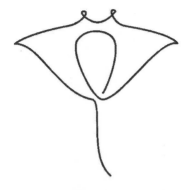

Thank you for reading this book. I hope you enjoyed reading it as much as I enjoyed writing it. Please consider leaving a review on Amazon or Goodreads. Reviews and ratings are the lifeblood of independent authors.

www.pepperbooks.org

Made in the USA
Middletown, DE
10 December 2021

55049682R00161